I, Barabbas

I, Barabbas

EDWARD BELL

RESOURCE *Publications* • Eugene, Oregon

I, BARABBAS

Resource Publications
An Imprint of Wipf and Stock Publishers
199 W. 8th Ave., Suite 3
Eugene, OR 97401

www.wipfandstock.com

PAPERBACK ISBN: 978-1-6667-1673-3
HARDCOVER ISBN: 978-1-6667-1674-0
EBOOK ISBN: 978-1-6667-1675-7

AUGUST 4, 2021

Contents

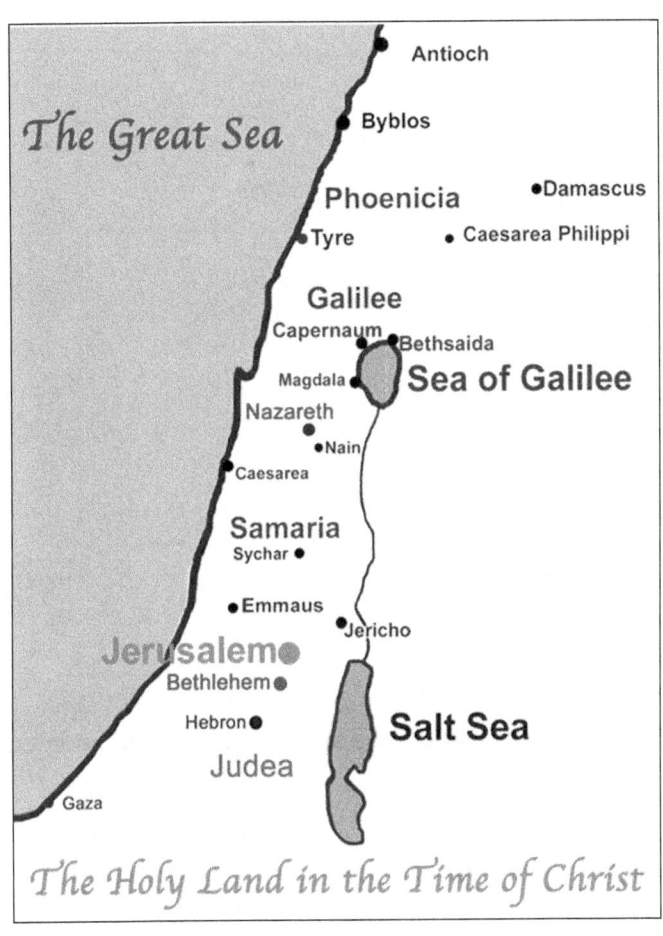

The Holy Land in the Time of Christ

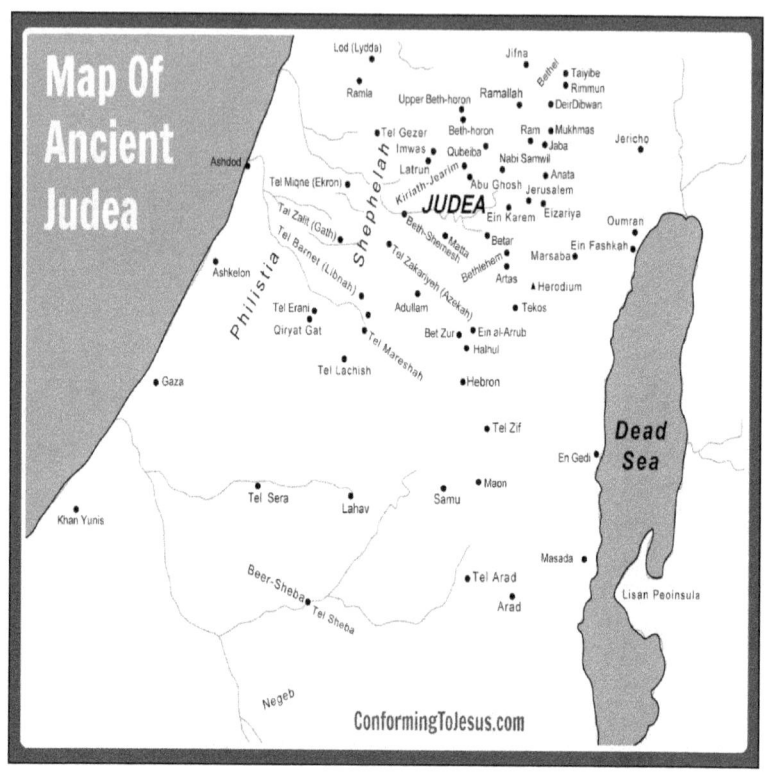

TOO LATE. I'M TOO late! My life was spared because of this man and now, when I've come to return the favor, I'm too late. I don't know why it's bothering me like this, because he was nothing more than another Jew, and I've killed my share of them over the years but something about this man is different, something I can't quite put my finger on. In the forty-seven years I've been alive I've killed many men and none of their deaths ever bothered me.

Maybe it was his eyes. They were a very deep penetrating hazel that seemed to look at and through you at the same time, and yet, they were very kind eyes. They were eyes that said I can see your faults but I don't cast blame. Looking up at the man now, his eyes were closed, appearing peaceful and yet they lacked life. Like a candle that shines brightly, the incredible darkness that ensues when it is snuffed out, the end to his countenance left utter darkness on all those gathered around him.

I found my heart breaking because of this man and I didn't even know him. I felt guilty but knew I wasn't responsible for his predicament. How could I be, I hadn't done anything to him. The people had made their choice and they were responsible.

I couldn't brush the thought of his eyes out of my mind. I think the only other time I had met anyone with eyes as penetrating was almost ten years ago in Salim when I first joined the rebellion.

CHAPTER ONE

I CAME FROM THE town of Nain, and at thirty-six years of age was always looking for a fight. Needless to say, I usually found one and because of my never-give-up attitude, I almost always won. If it appeared I was about to lose, I didn't hesitate to pull the fig knife I kept in my boot. Because of this attitude, at least seven men (that I know of) lost their lives.

It wasn't very long until my violent attitude and reputation were well known throughout the land and most people went out of their way to stay out of mine. I wasn't accustomed to any stranger just walking up to me demanding my attention. So you may well understand my anger and shock when a very large Samaritan approached me without even so much as inquiring if it was all right to do so.

Babbukiah was very large for a Samaritan, standing over four cubits tall and weighing around one hundred and thirty-six kilograms. With a hard, ruddy, and wind-weathered complexion, his many facial scars lent credence to his having seen a fair share of fights.

His large hands had the calluses that belong to hard-working men everywhere, but they also carried the distinct impression and depressions of having met with many teeth. As a warrior myself, I immediately assessed Babbukia's persona and stature and was shocked to find a growing apprehension as to whether I could beat *this man in a one-on-one fight. The more I looked at him, the more I was certain I could not.*

It was with great trepidation that I watched him approach. Suddenly, he broke into a wide grin. "Barabbas, isn't it?" He asked.

Now I was taken aback. This man knew my name. I looked down to see he had extended his hand in a friendly gesture of the customary handshake. Cautiously I accepted his hand and immediately noticed it was as gnarled and rough as a rock and his grip would have had me wincing had I not been determined to show no sign of weakness.

"My name is Babbukia," he continued. "And while you don't know me, I have heard a great deal about you, Barabbas."

I hadn't spoken yet because I was still confused and I hated to admit, a little intimidated. "I feel it's safe for me to tell you, I am with a band of men who openly oppose the Empire and your story travels well throughout the land. In some places, you are considered a hero, and others, well, let's just say, the price on your head makes you a lucrative target." Babbukia explained.

Not knowing this man and having him tell me this made me wonder his intention and left me looking around for a way to escape. I had no way of knowing his true intent and wasn't sure I wanted to wait around to find out.

"Easy, big guy," Babbukia said confidently, as if reading my thoughts." I can tell you don't trust me, but I can assure you, I mean you no harm. On the contrary, I think we can be of beneficial help to one another."

The look in his eyes said 'trust me,' but my life had taught me never to trust anyone, especially anyone who knew this much about me.

"Okay, so you know who I am, now what is it you want?" I asked.

"As I said, I'm here as a member of a group of people whose sole reason for existence is to eliminate the empire by any means necessary," Babbukia said looking around nervously. "You would be of great service to the people if you were to join us."

Of great service to the people? And why would I be interested in doing anything for the people, the people had never done anything for me and they had always considered me an outlaw, an outcast.

It was five years earlier, and I was a simple carpenter who made an adequate living making furniture and repairing boats. I also maintained a small herd of sheep that my eight-year-old son, Dodavah shepherded. I enjoyed an excellent family life along with my son and beautiful wife, Rebekah. I could not have been happier and felt on top of the world. One day I heard a large supply of teakwood had arrived in Megiddo from the Far East and besides being a very hardwood, it made beautiful furniture. Packing for the trip, I explained to Rebekah that I would also be in the market for several ewes for breeding purposes.

Walking across our field, I spotted Dodavah amongst the herd and called to him. Upon hearing my voice, he broke into a run, and as he got closer I could see a wide smile. My heart swelled with pride. While he had many of his mother's features, he was a quick learner and had taken to carpentry and shepherding with an enthusiasm similar to mine.

"Listen, son. I must go on a trip to buy some wood for our craft. I should be gone no more than four days." I explained. "While I am gone, I want you to keep an eye on everything and do whatever your mother says. Will you do that for me?"

"Yes, Papa," Dodavah answered. His eyes were downcast and troubled. "Why can't I go with you, Papa?"

"Well, if you go with me, who will watch over your mother?" I asked. "She needs a man about for tasks and protection. Do you understand?" I could see his little chest swelling with pride over the expected manly duties I was leaving him with. "I will watch over everything Papa."

In Megiddo, I successfully bargained for ten cords of teak, ten cords of pine, and fifteen ewes and was on my way home when I stopped at the small town of Cathron to water the oxen and enjoy a cool drink of date wine. A crowd was gathered at the town's only inn and seemed very agitated. Both men and women were crying the same question, "Why?"

"What happened? Why is everyone so upset and crying?" I asked.

"The Legionnaires came through and killed many of our people, took our herds, crops, and the few denarii some of us were able to save."

"And from which direction did these Legionnaires come?" I asked.

"They carried the standard of Cadara." Came the reply.

I had feared the answer because to get to Cathron from Cadara meant the Legionnaires would have to go through Nain.

I left the oxen, which carried the wood and the sheep with some of the town's citizens. Borrowing a donkey, I made a quick exit out of town for home. I could only hope the worst had not happened.

Cresting a hill that overlooked our land, I could see smoke rising in the distance and knew then my worst fear would undoubtedly be realized. Kicking the donkey harder than the poor animal was used to, I rushed down the hill only to discover the smoke was coming from what used to be our home.

At the smoking ruined shell that had once been a happy family abode, I could easily make out the bodies of Dodavah and Rebekah, their skin a ghostly pale white against the gray of smoldering ash. I didn't have to touch them to know they were dead, but I had to. I had to hold their broken bodies close to mine as if to absorb any flickering life that may not have ebbed away. My eyes welled with tears that almost wiped away the ghastly sight before me. I felt as broken as anyone could feel. Dodavah and Rebekah were my whole life, the only reason I lived and without them, I wasn't sure I even wanted to live.

Why? Who could do such a thing? Anyone could see these two were not a threat of any kind, to anyone. Finding a large stick, I began to scrape at the hard earth in the feeble attempt to make their graves.

Seeing the unclothed and obscene position they had left Rebekah in, left no doubt as to what happened. Seeing Dodavah close by his mother, told me he had made a valiant attempt to perform the duties I had charged him with to the very end.

Something within me snapped and life suddenly didn't matter anymore. I vowed then and there, over the bodies of my family, I would do everything possible to make those who had committed these atrocities pay dearly.

While I had no way of knowing which Legionnaire was responsible, it didn't matter, in my eyes, they were all equally guilty. The entire Roman Empire was guilty and I was determined to make it pay. I realized it would mean my death, but without my family, life was not worth living anyway.

The first Legionnaire to feel my wrath was innocently enough retrieving his stallion from a Smith. He was bartering payment for work done when I crept up behind him. Slowly drawing a knife from the folds of my robe, I was about to thrust the blade into the Legionnaire's back when the Smith yelled, "Hey, what do you think you're doing?"

The Smith's question served as a warning to the Roman and he quickly whirled about to face me, sword drawn in one smooth move. My reflexes were faster and I quickly plunged my knife into his torso just below the heart under the rib cage. Death was reflected in the soldier's eyes as recognition of his fate etched into his dying brain. The only sound to escape him was the rancid rush of his final breath and then he fell at my feet.

I was startled out of my shocked stupor by a panicked yell from the Smith. He was screaming at anyone who would listen, that a murder had just occurred. It didn't take long before the curious began to approach the Smith's shop and I knew it wouldn't be long before the rest of the Legionnaire's unit came running from the inn.

As I turned to run, hands grabbed me about the waist and almost knocked me to the ground. I attempted to break the Smith's grip, but he was too strong from the many years of caring for and shoeing horses. With the knife still in hand, I quickly pushed it into one of the arms that had captured me. The Smith let out a blood-curdling scream and released his grip. Fearing he would again grab me, I again plunged the knife into the Smith, but this time I stabbed him in the throat. Attempting to scream, the only sound the Smith was able to produce was a liquid-sounding gurgle as his life ebbed and then he was lying next to the Legionnaire. I didn't hesitate and ran from the Smith's shop, found the donkey, and quickly rode away before other Legionnaires arrived.

I knew I was doomed because too many of the townspeople had seen me and under interrogation, would provide a good description. I also had no doubt some in town knew me from previous trips, so I had no choice but to run and keep running. As I fled town an almost incomprehensible feeling of exhilaration exuded through me. I wouldn't equate it with the satisfaction I had felt taking life, but more from the power of revenge.

CHAPTER TWO

"AND JUST WHY, WOULD I be interested in joining your band of . . . of what, outlaws, thieves?" I asked Babbukia.

"Not thieves, Barabbas, revolutionaries. We have a cause that requires us to rebel against the empire." Babbukia explained. "And we know, from your actions and some of the statements you've made in the past, that you are no friend of the empire. Besides, as you know, your freedom is very limited. The empire's Legions know all about you and are out looking for you now. It's only a matter of time before they come for you. Now, you can simply wait until they come and end up in a dungeon awaiting death; try to outrun them and prolong your certain death, or you can join us and make a difference."

"Make a difference?" I interrupted. "Make a difference how? What can we do against Pilate and his men that would make any kind of difference? No, I'm leaving. Your talk is of rebellion and they execute you for rebelling against the Roman Empire."

"All right, Barabbas, go," Babbukia said calmly. "You're already a marked man and in time, they will get you, and believe me, you will be executed. With us, they may still get you, but at least you have a fighting chance. But go, I understand, go ahead and run. I wish you well."

Babbukia turned to leave. I realized I would have to make a decision quickly because once he was gone, I was sure I would never see him again. The question was, do I stay a loner as I had always been since leaving Nain, relying on my own instincts to survive or, do I join him and at least make an attempt at revolution. If worse came to worse, I would still be executed but at least for a cause. At best, the people would join us in revolt, and then what? I didn't have the answer but I was certain that alone my time was limited at best.

"Wait. Babbukia!" I yelled at the receding figure.

Slowly turning to face me, he waited until I approached extending his hand again then he broke into a wide grin.

"Welcome Barabbas, you've made the right decision. Now let's go and meet the others."

That was eleven years ago. At first, it seemed we were truly making progress as people from the villages of Nain, Megiddo, Beth Shan, and as far away as Gadara joined the rebellion. Our numbers swelled from a ragtag outfit of forty to a formidable guerilla force of fifteen hundred men. Even the women and children were taught to fight to the death, so this made our number even greater. All for naught.

How could we have been so stupid? As the Roman governor over all Judea, Pilate kept two-hundred-twenty thousand Legionnaires at his access, as well as one- hundred twenty-five thousand Royal Imperial Guards within the city of Jerusalem. If he required it, he could easily call upon neighboring governors to lend him an additional four-hundred thousand Legionnaires to squash any resistance we might mount.

Babbukia and I traveled to the coastal town of Caesarea where we met up with the others. I must admit, at first I was petrified at what I saw. A loose, very loose group of men, women, and children who looked malnourished, dirty, and whipped. What I was quick to learn was what they didn't have in equipment, training, and numbers, they more than made up for by possessing the heart of a warrior. In short, these people could, would and did fight.

Our first raiding party occurred at the town of Aenon, north of Salim along the Jordan River. We had sent spies out a month earlier, we were aware the town housed a contingent of four hundred

Legionnaires. While they were better equipped, we carried the element of surprise in our arsenal.

We left Caesarea headed due east to Beth Shan where we followed the Jordan River south to Salim. Arriving around midnight, it seemed the entire town's population (except for Legion perimeter guards) seemed to be asleep. A fifteen-foot high wall, made from boulders taken from the nearby mountainside encircled the entire town. Unfortunately for the sleeping town's citizens, these boulders afforded us an easy means with which to scale the walls.

Babbukia assigned twenty of our strongest, agile warriors to scale the wall to eliminate the guards. Because I had always prided myself on staying healthy, I quickly volunteered for this task and was just as quickly put in charge of our assault team.

Slowly making our way up the wall in the cover of darkness, the ascent was surprisingly easy with the boulder's rough texture serving as an adequate hand and footholds. Cresting the top of the wall, we cautiously peered over and immediately saw the wall had been built with a catwalk encircling the top that afforded the guards the ability to observe the town's streets while permitting a clear line of sight over the surrounding countryside.

Easing our way over the wall onto the catwalk, my heart was banging in my chest as we awaited the blare of a Legionnaire trumpet that we were certain would come, effectively alerting the other soldiers their enclosure had been breached, but it never came. It appeared, in addition to the town's people being asleep, those assigned to guard duty were either gambling, drinking, or themselves asleep on duty. The first guard to be dispatched was seated in a chair at the top of a staircase that led to the town's main square. He seemed to be half-heartedly interested in a drunken man attempting to accost an equally drunken woman.

Approaching the guard from the back, two of our men quickly grabbed and subdued him. The first grabbing the guard across the face with hands incapacitating his ability to breath, much less cry out. The second quickly drew a knife across the guard's throat. With a steady flow of blood running over his arms, the first warrior firmly held the guard's head still against the inevitable death throes. When there was no further movement, he let the Legionnaire's body fall to the catwalk.

The second warrior signaled the rest of us it was all right to continue our assault on the wall. Easing the rest of the way over the wall, our confidence was building, as we met no resistance. Instead of accuracy, our confidence meant carelessness.

Looking back in retrospect, the smart thing to do would have been to post some of our own guards to serve as a warning system lest we be surprised. We failed miserably in this area as every man in our raiding party dropped the ten feet from the catwalk onto the square. The minute the last of our party was safely on the ground, doors from the surrounding buildings burst open, and in an instant, we were trapped in the middle of what seemed to be the entire Roman Legion.

A bloody battle ensued with our party losing almost half its warriors, while the Legionnaires lost approximately one hundred, a small percentage in comparison. The rest of our group was quickly subdued, arrested, and taken to the dungeons to await trial before Governor Pontius Pilate. Each of us shared in the knowledge death was imminent, as Emperor Caesar had decreed that any form of rebellion or insurrection against the empire was punishable by death and governors like Pilate took great delight in executing that decree. Over the next four days, seven-hundred and forty-eight of our party was taken to the Praetorium and presented to Pilate as insurrectionists and just as quickly sentenced to death.

CHAPTER THREE

NOT EVERYONE RECEIVED THE *same death sentence of course, as that would have been too boring for Pilate. Throughout the Roman Empire, he was well known for the exceptionally cruel ways in which he dispatched his enemies. If he could make the executions a form of entertainment for the citizens of the Empire, all the better.*

Two of our men Crispus and Antioch were forced to fight each other to the death using crudely made maces that were studded through with pointed spikes. As soon as Crispus dispatched Antioch, he stood over the defeated warrior and in agony cried out his shame. His agony was short-lived as a Legionnaire thrust him through with a spear on orders from Pilate.

Others were forced to fight wild animals, of which some had been brought to Judea from parts unknown, on the whim they would delight Pilate in their animalistic assault on human flesh. There were tigers, lions, and packs of dogs called Devil Dogs from Ethiopia, hyenas, wild boars, and more than once, bears were brought in. If it appeared one of our men would defeat an animal, immediately two more animals of the same kind would be released from the very bowels of the Praetorium so the man would quickly be outnumbered and overcome.

And then there was Eran. He was twenty-three years of age with a quick wit and engaging smile. He was also very large, in fact, some described him as a mountain of a man. He had been one of our better wrestlers and the Legionnaires were well aware of his reputation. They worried he would defeat any animal put up against him, thereby inflaming others to resist. A special death was devised for Eran.

After going days without any light in our cells, those of us who hadn't been selected for death yet were brought up to the Praetorium's arena to watch what means of death Clausius (Captain of Pilates guard) had devised for Eran. As we waited, four gold-gilded chariots with teams of two white horses each were led onto the grounds. Aboard each chariot was an equally gold-gilded Legionnaire Charioteer. The entryway to the arena known as the Gate of the Condemned was raised and Eran was led in.

It was easy to see he had been physically abused and had great difficulty walking. Around each of his wrists and ankles were shackles that were fastened to very large chains. Even though each chain's end was held by a Legionnaire, the weight of the chain's slack almost forced Eran to his knees. Eran was led to the center of the arena and waited while the chariots circled closer and closer menacingly around him. At first, we thought they intended to trample him to death. What they had in mind was worse.

Each chariot with its team of horses was stopped and aligned in the four directions of the city, which placed one team each a short distance from Eran's arms and legs. When the chariots were in position, the Legionnaires who held the ends of each chain helped the charioteers affix them to the back of the chariots. When they finished securing the ends, each Legionnaire took his turn pummeling Eran until he could stand no longer and fell in a cloud of dust and dried animal dung. All four charioteers looked to the gallery in the direction of Pilate. With an ever-widening grin, Pilate didn't hesitate to thrust his hand out before him and gave a thumbs down signal, indicating the proceedings should continue.

The charioteers took up whips and coaxed their team of horses into a slow, steady walk, stretching the slack out of each chain. Slowly, Eran's broken body began to rise into the air, as the chain's slack became taunt. With recognition, those gathered grew quiet as it became apparent what was about to happen to Eran. The whips cracked against the backs of each team of horses and the assaulted steeds lunged forward in an attempt to establish a gait. The quiet was suddenly broken by Eran's long agonizing scream. He was the nucleus at which each chariot was tethered. Against the equine strength, his body was not able to withstand and began to be pulled in four directions.

As the horses fought against each other, Eran's body was slowly pulled apart. His anguished screams did not stop until he had been ripped into four parts and then the arena went quiet. The only sound to be heard was the snorting of the horse's nostrils. The rest of us captives could do nothing but weep. Not so much for Eran, but at our own fates. Were we too, to be torn apart like an old rag or ravaged by wild animals? I began to wonder if this rebellion had been worth it. What had I gained? We were fighting against a system that had existed for hundreds of years. Did we think we could change anything?

As the sun began to fade, Pilate determined it was too dark to proceed with any more games for the day so we were returned to our cells in the dungeons. On the way to my cell, I passed before another that was occupied by a strange man who was not part of the rebellion, yet he drew as much if not more attention than we did. While we spent our confinement time screaming and cursing the guards, this man did nothing and made no sound. Rumor from some of the guards was he spent most of his time in prayer. It was also rumored the strange man was some sort of King and because of that, he was a threat to Cesar. Whatever or whoever he was, he never made a sound.

The next morning we were awakened by the sound of many Legion boots. Startled from sleep, we stood and awaited their arrival at our cells and escort to the arena, but it never came. Instead, the Legionnaires stopped at the cell of the strange man.

We could hear the loud commands and cursing as they roused the man from sleep. Then the unmistakable sound of punches could be heard. Over and over, the man was beaten, ridiculed, and spit on, and yet, he did nothing to resist, nor did he cry out. We had heard he was the leader of another rebellious group but he was the only one to get caught. What I found strange was the rumor his army consisted *of former fishermen and while I knew men who hunted the seas were hard men and known to fight, they were not of an army caliber and it was no wonder their leader was captured. Rumor also held that his people would make a grand stand to liberate their leader and when they did, all of us would also be freed.*

I know I wasn't alone in my thinking, if this man's group could free us, I would do all I could to join them. From that moment I made it a vow, if the opportunity presented itself, I would find a way to talk to the man and find out more. I didn't have long to wait. That evening, another man became ill and went into convulsions, which required the two guards on duty to remove him from his cell. One thing about Pilate, he refused to have any prisoner die without his having a hand in their demise. This meant medical treatment long enough for the afflicted prisoner to be the next mornings entertainment in the arena.

As the sound of guard boots melted into the distance I took my chance to contact the prisoner down the wing.

"Hey. Hey, you down the walk, are you awake?"

I didn't receive a reply and tried again, speaking a little louder as I realized the guards would be outside the range of hearing anything down here.

"Can you hear me? You in the first cell, can you hear me?" I had to hold my breath to hear the faint response, but it was a response.

"I can hear you." The man answered.

"I am here for rebellion and they told me at the trial I am to be executed. Of course, I use the term trial loosely, I was going to be guilty before I even went before Pilate." I offered. "What are you in for?"

"Like you Barabbas, I've been charged with rebellion and violation of the laws. And while I have not been before Pilate yet, I know I too will be executed."

I was taken aback. I had not mentioned my name to this unseen stranger and yet, he distinctly called me by my name.

"How do you know my name and how come you were the only one captured? How many are in your group?" I asked. "Did someone tell on you?"

"There were thirteen of us and . . . "

"Thirteen?" I questioned in disbelief. "The word around here is you're the leader of a rebellious group and you're telling me there are only thirteen of you? Everyone here believes your group will be coming to rescue you and we will be freed as well."

"It was not written that I was to be rescued, but that I must die for the sins of others." The man stated flatly.

"So because of others' faults, you have to take the blame? And I suppose someone betrayed you?" I inquired.

Like any group, you always have those who are cowards and traitors. Talk throughout the dungeon had it that one of his most trusted friends had betrayed him while he was praying.

"Yes, and yes again." The man answered. "One of my closest friends made a deal to hand me over. When the Legionnaires came to arrest me, I was the only one they had come for so the others got away."

"Wait a minute," I stated incredulously, "you're telling me you have a group of rebels, and the minute Legionnaires come for you, their leader, the others tum and run? I mean, they didn't fight or anything?"

"Make no mistake about it, they would have fought but I stopped them." He answered. "It was not written that violence would be used to achieve the cause, but on the contrary, love will win in the end. Now, that's not to say blood was not shed before my arrest. Before my being chained, one of my friends did strike out against a Legionnaire and seriously wounded him, but I had to stop him and the others before they too were arrested."

"So, are the others going to take care of the traitor? You know, get even for turning you in?" I asked. *I guess I was expecting to hear about some plan for payback however, what I got was more placid responses.*

"No, I would never have them commit violence on my behalf or for any other cause," He confessed timidly. "No, to issue statements of revenge is not mine to do. Besides, the man who betrayed me realized his wrongful actions and took his own life."

I was beside myself with anger at this unseen pacifist. He knew he was going to die and yet, and yet . . . he was acting just like his betraying friend, a coward. He was going to die, just like the rest of us and he seemed warm to the idea. I had had enough and asked no more questions and he offered no more explanations. Easing down to the straw on my cell floor, I attempted to go to sleep but sleep eluded me. All I could think about was the man's responses and the insanity of it all. He was the leader of a band of rebels that bothered Pilate a great deal but he was not going to issue orders to attempt a rescue.

More confusing, how could his men just let him stay here in this repository of the damned knowing that to do so meant sure death for their leader? And yet there was something about this man that instilled both fear and calm within me. His voice stayed calm with an air of authority to it and even without seeing him, I could understand why someone would have the confidence to follow such a person. His voice made me feel anything was possible.

Chapter Four

I was aroused from my thoughts by the jangle of keys. A thin sliver of light through a crack in the wall convinced me morning had arrived. Unfortunately, this also meant the torment would continue for some unlucky soul. Was that soul to be me?

The sound of boots resounded throughout the cavernous dungeon and it echoed like the whole Legion was descending into its bowels. My heart began to race with fear and my mouth became dry, yet a cold sweat broke out on my brow. I was certain they had come for me but admittedly, felt relief when they stopped at the strange man's cell.

"Hey! Hey you, King of the Jews," they yelled. "Wake up. It's your turn to go in front of Pilate."

The very rapid and loud sounds of thuds emanated from the cell as the unmistakable sound of boots hitting flesh bounced off the dungeon's walls. Besides a loud expelling of air, like someone had been kicked in the stomach, no other sound came from the cell.

"Get up!" a Legionnaire screamed. "Pilate may not be a King like you, but as governor, he's not accustomed to being kept waiting." He mocked.

There were more slaps and punches with occasional grunts from both the issuer and receiver of the assaults. These repugnant sounds receded down the hall and eventually faded from my hearing.

I could only wonder what means of torture and death Pilate had devised for the strange man. One thing was certain, the physical assault he withstood would have forced almost any other man to wilt in a sobbing heap.

I knew the layout of Pilate's court and could almost see, in my mind's eye, the man being dragged to the open courtyard before hundreds of citizens gathered to gawk at the condemned. What confused me the most, was the overheard conversations by the guards and some of the other prisoners who referred to the Jew as a holy man and yet, it was the Jews who were clamoring for his conviction as much as the Romans.

My relief was short-lived. Not long after the sound of boots echoing down the hall had died away, they could be heard coming back and since there were only two cells in this hall, I surmised it was my turn. My trepidation grew intense as I tried to figure by which means I would meet my demise.

Pilate must have come up with something heinous and quick for the Jew because he hadn't lasted long. I was used to the death of Pilate's prisoners being all-day affairs at his pleasure. It must have been true, Pilate hated and was scared of the Jew and wanted him dead quick. But what did that mean for me?

The Legion commander called to me, "Barabbas, come to the front of your cell and don't try anything stupid, there are ten of us out here." *I slowly eased my way to the cell's door. As it creaked on the hinges, sunlight filtered through and assaulted my eyes. The cell was dark and the stream of light felt like a knife stabbing through my eyes to the back of my brain. My vision returned at about the same time that my legs seemed to fail. I stumbled through the door and almost fell but was held up by a very erect standing Legionnaire who seemed to delight in my inability.*

"Prisoner Barabbas, you are to be brought before the governor's court," *the commander stated militarily.* "The charges against you are insurrection against the Empire as a member of and/or establishing a rebellion. The punishment for these charges is death." *He nodded to the other Legionnaires, who promptly grabbed me by the arms and slammed me face-first against the wall. Holding a spear to the small of my back to ensure I did not move from the wall, they quickly fastened shackles to my wrists and ankles. It was apparent they hadn't realized, nor did they care that the apparatus was designed for a much smaller person. Their first attempts to close the shackles met with resistance, as my size would not permit them to be secured. With two Legionnaires now pushing on either side of each shackle, they succeeded in closing them. Blood oozed from my right wrist as the skin was unmercifully pinched and the tissue was torn loose.*

Chapter Five

As if I were some wild animal, they also locked a shackle around my throat that was attached to an extremely heavy chain. It left no doubt that I was going to go wherever the Legionnaires intended. With the spear still firmly pressed against my back, I was forced down the hall toward a fate I was all too certain meant an excruciatingly painful death. Along the corridor, I was forcefully kicked many times in the buttocks and thighs, on more than one occasion I had to be helped up. This too was accomplished very roughly and painfully. Finally, we arrived at the steps that led to the Praetorium's arena.

Climbing the steep, slippery incline that led into the arena, my confusion only intensified as a growing cacophony of angry human voices filled the air. On most days when entertainment was provided, there was much laughter and squeals of excitement as some macabre scene played out before them. This sound was distinctly the sound of angry people who were on the verge of unrest. Could this be because of me, I wondered. I know I am a wanted man and have a price on my head, but these people sounded like Baal himself had entered the arena.

In the open arena, I looked around and saw the gallery was filled with a mixture of Roman citizens and Jews alike. It certainly looked like the entire population of Judea and surrounding countryside was in attendance. Surely I am not that important to these *people, I surmised. As I was pushed to the far end of the arena, the appearance of Pilate's court could be seen.*

Seated upon a dais that overlooked the crowds, Pilate sat regally, and yet there was unmistakable anguish to his expression. On the platform where he sat, the regional commander of the Legionnaires stood in his finest gilded uniform. Surrounding the dais was a full regiment of Legionnaires ready and willing to die to protect the governor. You could feel their edginess and a general sense of fear that accompanies men who go to war. They were prepared for something and that something could not be good.

Another individual stood on the dais not far from Pilate. Slumped would be a better description except he was being propped up by two hefty Legionnaires who seemed to be covered in blood. As I drew closer, I was able to get a better look at the poor individual who was being forced to stand before this crowd. It became apparent as we snaked our way through this rabble that the anger this group was emanating was not being thrown in my direction because not once as we crossed the arena was I assaulted.

As I stood at the foot of the stairs that led to the dais I could see the individual a little better and what I saw could only be described as a horror. I have witnessed the deaths of many people and never have I seen so much blood or shredded skin. The man who stood there was a gaunt figure who was barely clothed in what appeared to be a loincloth and a blood-soaked robe of some kind. I could not see his musculature through the massive amount of blood that covered him. How could a man bleed that much and still be alive? I wondered.

At the top of the stairs, I was forced to stand next to this poor, pitiful soul. It was then that I got my first look at his face. He was distinctly Jewish and indistinguishable by most standards, except for the eyes. There was something about his eyes that bore through me as I stood next to him. His gaze made me feel guilty, but guilty of what. But there was something more being said through his eyes. They appeared to say, "my pain is about to end, but I feel so sorry for what you must come to endure." Suddenly, Pilate was on his feet, waving his hands to silence the crowd who immediately stilled.

Striding over to the Jew and myself, Pilate sauntered like a man who knows he has supreme power and intends to use it. With a voice that boomed within the cavernous Praetorium, Pilate stated,

"It is your custom for me to release one prisoner at the time of the Passover. Do you want me to release the King of the Jews, or this murderous traitor Barabbas? *As he asked this question, the quieted crowd erupted into screams and yells* "No, not him! Give us Barabbas!"

I couldn't believe my ears. I had forgotten it was the Passover because I didn't place much credence in the nonsense spoken by the Jews, but these people were yelling for my release at the expense of the man standing next to me and he was one of their own. Pilate again raised his hands for quiet and again inquired,

"Which of these prisoners do you want me to release to you, Barabbas, or Jesus who is called Christ?"

With one voice the crowd cried out, "Away with this man! Release Barabbas to us!"

What astounded me was not more than three days earlier, when this man I now knew was called Jesus rode into town, he was cheered and held up to be a savior for these wretched people. All their pain and suffering would end and good times were to come, and now, here they were screaming for this man's blood. What strange and fickle people, these Jews.

The trial of Jesus was very odd indeed. While I am not an attorney, I did speak with one who joined the rebellion because he had grown very disgruntled with the system and he explained why Jesus had been illegally convicted. Jesus faced charges before the Jewish Sanhedrin, which was the highest judicial and ecclesiastical council, composed of from seventy to seventy-two members. Various members of a Jewish sect known as Pharisees had brought specific charges against Jesus because they emphasized strict interpretation and observance of the Mosaic Law. Once a set of charges was determined to be adequate, they were presented to the Sadducee priests who in turn would write the charges for presentation to the court.

For the first time, something close to bewilderment registered on Pilate's face.

"Why? What crime has he committed?"

The crowd had grown frantic in its anger and discernible statements could not be understood.

The difficulty of Pilate's situation was evident by his earlier actions. While the Pharisees and Sadducees had brought Jesus to him to be sentenced for stirring up the people of Galilee, he saw an opportunity,

"Galilee? This man is a Galilean?" Pilate turned to his Commander of the Legion and asked, "Is Herod in Jerusalem?"

With that, he decided one with more power and accustomed to such matters should be made to handle the issue.

Jesus was sent to Herod Antipas who served as Emperor Tiberius Caesar's provisional Ruler of Judea and tetrarch in Galilee. As tetrarch, Herod was one of four joint rulers who issued edicts on behalf of the empire and because of an inflated and perverted ego, liked to embarrass and harass those brought before him for judgment. It was Herod's marriage to his niece Herodias that made news throughout the region and denounced by a religious zealot named John the Baptist, who was later beheaded at the urging of Salome, the daughter of Herod and Herodias.

I can imagine the relief Pilate must have felt sending Jesus to Herod, followed by the utter terror at having him sent right back. Word spread that Herod, after trying many tactics to get Jesus to perform some type of magic, or to speak on his own behalf, became frustrated and declared the Jew a lunatic and would not waste his time on the issue. The crowd had grown frantic in its anger and discernible statements could not be understood.

"What shall I do, then, with Jesus who is called Christ?" Pilate asked. He looked sick like he had eaten something spoiled. Almost to a person, the gathered screamed, "Crucify him!"

CHAPTER SIX

JEWISH LAW DICTATED DEATH sentences were to be carried out by stoning, beheading, or strangulation, and because of the charges against him, Jesus would have been sentenced to stoning. Crucifixion was strictly a Roman sentence and could not be applied to Jesus. The law also stated that before a death sentence could be imposed, two or more witnesses must come forward in total agreement as to the charges, or an acquittal had to be announced.

Two witnesses were brought before the court but they could not agree on any charges against Jesus, even to the extent of a statement that they asserted he made. One claimed Jesus stated, "I will destroy the temple." While the other stated he claimed, "I will destroy this temple." Repeatedly the high priests of the Sanhedrin, as well as Pilate himself asked Jesus to make statements that would effectively be admitting guilt. This too, was against Jewish law which stated an accused could not be forced to make statements against themselves. It was also explained that under Jewish law, the condemned could not be convicted by less than a unanimous vote, and someone must come forward on behalf of the charged to avoid the implementation of a death sentence. In Jesus' case, this was not accomplished.

As I scanned the crowd I could see it was the chief priests and elders who were persuading and provoking the crowd to ask for my release and to have this man, Jesus executed. I didn't know what to feel, I couldn't. I had never met this Jew but it was obvious everyone else knew who he was. The fact Pilate was having trouble deter-mining what to do intrigued me. Jesus had to be very important to generate these types of responses and yet, to look at him, he looked no more important than some poor vagrant would. I began to feel sympathy for him.

While I felt sorry for this man, I nonetheless was happy the peo-ple were calling for my release. Unless Pilate made an erratic change to his decree, I would be set free, but, then what? Uproar amongst the citizens was beginning to sound like it might turn violent. Address-ing his aide Pilate commanded, "Bring me a chalice of water and a vessel, so that I may clean my hands of this sordid mess." *When the aide returned, Pilate made a grand display by having his minion pour water over his hands in front of the gathered mob while noting,* "I am innocent of this man"s blood, it is your responsibility!"

In response, the people yelled, "Let his blood be on us and our children!" *Pilate turned to me and with a look of utter disgust stated,* "These people have spoken and I am bound to release you. This day, you are a very lucky man. Tomorrow will be another day and Barabbas, I can guarantee you I will not be as forgiving. If you know what is good for you, leave Judea and the surrounding countryside."

As a Legionnaire began to release the shackles from me, I heard Pilate give the commander of the Legion the order to have Jesus flogged, and handed over to the masses to be crucified. At the very thought of crucifixion my blood ran cold. I had witnessed three cru-cifixions and I can attest it is the cruelest form of execution one can imagine. The victim suffocates to death as the entire weight of their body makes the lifting process required to force the lungs to breathe impossible. It is a very slow and painful process. At times, however, if soldiers grow impatient or Pilate gives the order, they will break the victim's knees so they are no longer able to keep pushing themselves up and the suffocation process begins almost immediately. Dizziness and delirium ensue as blood from the upper body quickly rushes to the lower regions, driving many to go crazy in those final hours. Joints dislocate from the intense pressure and weakness is ensured due to the loss of blood where the spikes are driven into the wrists

and ankles. In all, the victim can languish for three or four days in
nothing but agony.

    My hands began to tingle as the blood rushed into them after
the removal of the too-tight shackles. Rubbing them to increase cir-
culation I was aghast to note I had rubbed the skin off. This no doubt
was the result of the shackles being too tight for too long. Looking up,
I found myself staring into the condemned man's eyes. Even though
he was undoubtedly a dead man, his gaze burned with the intensity
of life and I found it difficult to force my eyes away from him. His
cracked and bloody lips parted and he was barely able to whisper. I
leaned forward and was astounded at what he said. "Fear not, for I
go to make a place for you too, Barabbas. This is not of your making as it was foretold. I love you, my brother."

    I don't know why but I felt like crying. But crying for what,
because this stranger would be dead in a short while? Because he
had said he loved me? Or because by his conviction I would now
go free? I didn't know the answer but I was certain it was a little of
each. I looked out across the crowd and my legs almost involuntarily
broke into a crazed run. I was running because I was happy to be free
but also because I needed to get away from this madness. As I ran
through the masses, it was like I was invisible to the gathered. Their
angered stares were reserved for Jesus and Jesus alone. Everyone in
the region hated Pilate, yet this anger was different. This anger spoke
of something they felt as vile. Something needing to be eliminated.

    As I reached the edge of the gathering and realized I was not
being followed, I dared to turn and look back up at the dais. What I
saw was Jesus being led down the steps from the dais into the gather-
ing of insanity. He was repeatedly kicked, hit, spit upon, and stoned,
all to the delight of the Legionnaires escorting him.

    Just how strong was this Jesus? Each time he was felled by a
blow or thrown rock, he would push himself back up and begin walk-
ing to his death again. I was amazed. Such strength was usually only
seen amongst true warriors and Jesus was anything but. In time,
however, Jesus could no longer go on, let alone carry the cross. He
fell face down with the heavy burden of the cross falling onto him. He

made repeated efforts to push himself up but the beatings throughout the day had finally taken their toll.

The Roman guard in charge of the death walk, grew impatient, pummeling Jesus while spitting exhortations for him to get up. One of the Centurions beckoned a very large, black-skinned man I was later to learn was named Simon from the capital city of Cyrene in Cyrenaica, which is in northern Africa. The Cyrenian was being ordered to carry Jesus' cross and an argument developed. The Cyrenian and Centurion were on the verge of fighting when I watched the thin, blood-caked hand of Jesus inch across the rock-strewn road toward the Cyrenian's barefoot. At the instant Jesus' hand touched him, the African's countenance changed.

What had been a face filled with the unmistakable expression of anger, the Cyrenian's visage was now replaced by an almost peaceful countenance. Balancing the cross on his back with one hand, the Cyrenian used his other to help Jesus to his feet. Slowly both men made their way out of town to the hill of execution. The hill which overlooked the city simultaneously allowed the citizens to see the condemned and hear their screams and cries of agony. Romans believed Golgotha was the answer and deterrent to rebellion. What they didn't know was watching so many of their countrymen executed in such a ghastly fashion only served to incite the population to join groups bent on revolt. It was just such a group I was led to believe that Peter was encouraging me to join.

I learned that like myself, Jesus was a carpenter by trade as had been his father before him. Somewhere along the line he became deluded into thinking he was the hoped-for Messiah the Jews prayed for and anxiously awaited. It was this attitude that so angered the Jewish elders that they decided the man must die. That was the main reason I didn't hold to accepting any of the religious concepts that ran rampant through the country. There were as many gods and goddesses as there were leaders to persuade them and each had very real and threatening repercussions if you violated the laws associated with them.

I, Barabbas

As for me, I didn't need some hoped-for Messiah to liberate and save me. I knew the only way to break the bonds of servitude and live a better life was to take what was needed to accomplish it.

CHAPTER SEVEN

As I watched Jesus being led away, I couldn't help but wonder how he had allowed himself to be placed in such a predicament. Everyone knew that rebellion meant sure death and because of that, most people conducted rebellious efforts in secret, but Jesus and his followers came riding into town boldly, being proclaimed each step of the way as the people's savior, all the while knowing it would generate wrath.

But Jesus had to be one of the bravest or craziest men I ever heard of. And what about his followers? His followers I heard were ordinary, simple and hard working people. Poor by Roman standards of living, but hard-working and in most cases, law abiding citizens. What would go through a man's mind to cause him to simply give up everything he has to follow an obvious zealot making wild claims and doing magic? Some of these men, I learned, had wives and children, and they just simply up and left them behind to follow this Jesus.

After his crucifixion, I learned more about Jesus' outfit, and what I found, made absolutely no sense. None of the men who followed him had ever been in a dungeon, let alone arrested. How did Jesus think he was going to overthrow the Roman Empire? I met a man several days after the crucifixion who told me he was one of Jesus' disciples, his name was Philip and he said he originally followed another zealot, also now dead, named John the Baptist. He said John told him he should be following this Jesus. He also said after meeting

Jesus, he felt compelled to follow the man blindly, without question. Philip said one of the first to follow was a fisherman named Simon Peter, he was the most outspoken of the group who had a brother named Andrew who also left everything to follow Jesus.

Another fisherman, who was in business with his younger brother John, was James. These four men gave up their fishing businesses to follow Jesus and become, as Philip put it, "fishers of men." John was the disciple I most wanted to meet. Philip said Jesus felt so much love for John it seemed to everyone who watched them, they were brothers. John was the only disciple who had not hidden and was present at the crucifixion. Bartholomew, who was also known as Nathanael was personally invited by Phillip to meet Jesus. Bartholomew was so overwhelmed at meeting Jesus, he began proclaiming the Jew was truly the Son of God.

Matthew, who was also called Levi, had worked as a tax collector, so he knew what it felt like to be hated. He had the most to lose by following Jesus as far as personal possessions were concerned. He left his very lucrative (and corrupt) profession to follow Jesus. This also prompted the Pharisees and Sadducees to condemn Jesus for mixing with "scum."

Philip said a man named Thomas had doubted Jesus from the very beginning, however, because he was friends of Simon Peter and Andrew, he didn't want to be left out in case there was some profit to be made in following Jesus around for a little while. There was another Simon, only he was called the Zealot. He was a political patriot who had become a follower of Jesus but managed to keep his nationalistic zeal.

Philip further explained, two of the more recent followers he knew very little about. All he knew about James was that he was the son of someone named Alphaeus, and even less was known about Thaddaeus, who was also known as Judas. Philip was very careful to point out that Thaddaeus was not to be confused with the last disciple he mentioned, Judas Iscariot. It seems Judas Iscariot was despicable to the other disciples from the very beginning. They didn't trust him and often told Jesus this, but they said their leader claimed

Judas was necessary to their cause as his lies and deceptions had been foretold long ago.

Philip said they learned later that Judas had betrayed Jesus for a mere thirty pieces of silver. Judas had a change of heart after Jesus was tried and felt so guilty, he hung himself. I found myself feeling good about that outcome.

It would seem Jesus' disciples felt more comfortable being part of a small group of twelve men. A vote was taken and of the many people, who routinely followed Jesus and his disciples, a man named Matthias was chosen to replace Judas.

How do you run a rebellion with only twelve rebels? This didn't make any sense to me. Philip told me they all knew they were doomed from the very beginning. When I asked him what the Jew felt about all this, Phillip stated Jesus was well aware of their situation and almost welcomed it.

It was two days before the Passover Festival, Phillip said and The Feast of Unleavened Bread, which begins the Passover celebration, was drawing near. Jesus told his disciples, "The Passover celebration begins in two days, and I will be betrayed and crucified."

Apparently at the same time Jesus was speaking, the leading priests, teachers of the law, and other leaders were meeting at the residence of Caiaphas, the high priest, to plot Jesus' murder. They were still looking for an opportunity to capture him and put him to death. For the life of me, I could not figure out how the others could continue to follow a man who so adamantly predicted his own death. All Philip could say was, "You would have had to have known him and felt his power." *It should be understood, during Jesus' short life, revolts against the Romans ran rampant and many false Messiahs emerged leading all manner of rebellions, only to be crushed in ruthless crackdowns.*

Jews were so desperate for the long-awaited prophet they traveled great distances to see a wild man in the desert who ate only locusts and honey, thinking that may be the hoped for Messiah. Every Jewish prophet teaches that someday a King would establish his kingdom, and that is the basis of rumors which so inflame the Jewish hope. When Jesus arrived you can imagine some of their disappointment when the mountains didn't tremble or enemies quiver with fear. He didn't come close to satisfying their extravagant hopes.

Philip spent all of that day, night, and into the next morning excitedly telling me some of the wildest stories I had ever heard, and he believed them, said he had personally witnessed some feats of magic he called miracles. Supposedly Jesus had cured blind and deaf people and could touch lepers without himself becoming leprous. I explained to him I had seen many festival tricksters who could do as much and magic was no reason to follow anyone. Philip was careful to explain it was nothing like that, Jesus was not a charlatan but a religious teacher and that he met all the Jewish expectations that a great deliverer would be born. He tried to convince me that it was Jesus, the prophet Isaiah predicted would be born of a virgin.

"Philip, you have to watch what you're saying," I warned. "Those kinds of statements will have the priest wanting your head next."

I was surprised by his response. After the trial, conviction, and crucifixion of Jesus, his men (except for Peter), had run away and even Peter, when confronted about his knowledge, denied knowing Jesus or the others and quickly ran and hid. It was well known Herod had decreed anyone with knowledge of or in allegiance to the Jew was to be arrested. "I know that," Phillip replied. "And it's true, at first we all felt certain we'd made a mistake and had followed a madman, and would probably pay with our lives. But I tell you Barabbas, since that horrible day they murdered him, I've seen things you could never believe or imagine. We are so sure of who Jesus is that none of us fears anymore.``

"You're just as crazy as he was," I injected.

"I'll tell you what Barabbas, why don't you come with me?"

"Go with you where?" I interrupted. *I had barely escaped execution once and I was not anxious to be put in that situation again.*

"Listen, I understand your fear," Phillip tried assuring me. "But I promise you, we'll be alright. The rest of us, except Judas . . . "

"Ah yes, Judas, the betrayer. Hung himself, right?"

"Yes, yes he did," Phillip, replied. "But this is not about Judas. All of us will be gathered for a meeting. It will be in broad daylight in a small room overlooking the town square."

"Why should I go? Why should I put myself in jeopardy like that?" I asked. *I realized I was looking about nervously, waiting to be arrested at any moment.*

"Because," Phillip responded. "All of your questions, spoken and felt will be answered. Then you can decide if the others and I are crazy. What about it, Barabbas?"

Chapter Eight

I followed Jesus as he was being led away by a command of Legionnaires through the city to the outskirts of town. I knew where they were headed because some in the crowd had mentioned he would be crucified at the "Skull." This was the name ominously given to a hill otherwise called Golgotha, and was visible from some distance away, serving as a hoped-for deterrent to anyone with the desire to oppose the empire. The road leading to Golgotha was lined with the wooden poles of prior crucifixions. Some still held men crying out in agony while affixed to them, while others still held fast the corpses of those left dangling for all to see. Others bore the skeletons of those whose flesh had rotted, or been picked away by carrion-eating birds and animals.

By crucifying Jesus atop the Skull, the Pharisees and Sadducees were making a statement for all to see. In essence, they were announcing, "don't mess with us and do not make claims to be something you're not, especially if it threatens our authority and income, because we will put you to death."

It was widely known throughout the countryside that both groups, Pharisees and Sadducees were involved in many illegal activities that generated ill-gotten gains. This, it was said, was one of the major reasons Jesus had openly challenged them. It seemed he had claimed one of the markets as belonging to his family and had become quite upset when he saw transactions taking place within and went on a one-man destruction endeavor, turning over gambling tables, and opening cages that held prized animals and fowl.

Forced to carry poles for their own crucifixion were two men from Lydda. While they weren't part of the rebellion, I had known both of them casually for many years. For the most part, Linus and Dalphon were small-time thieves, stealing produce from the town bazaars, as well as the occasional sheep left unattended. It was, however; their misfortune to have stolen some denarius from the purse of a Legionnaire who had drunk too much. He was drunk, but still capable of fighting and because of that and his desire to keep his earnings, resulted in his death.

Prior to their crucifixion walk, both men were in the dungeons with us and while Dalphon spent most of his time yelling and cursing, Linus spent hours crying because of his fate, wondering what would become of his family. He was leaving behind a wife and six children.

As Dalphon, Linus and Jesus made their way through the throngs that had gathered to watch their crucifixion, they were routinely hit with sticks, stones, insults, and spittle, but the worst abuse was reserved for Jesus. It seemed most in the crowd had a sincere hatred for the man and was beside themselves with anger. Such was their anger I wondered if he would be ripped to pieces before arriving at Golgotha.

Of the three, only Jesus was made to carry an already fashioned cross in the form of those used for crucifixions. Dalphon and Linus carried the customary cross beam that would be nailed to the top of a pole that stood upright vertically with one end sunk into the ground to keep it erect. The upright pole stood three hundred and sixteen cubits high with a crossbeam of one hundred forty-four cubits long. The crossbeam would be nailed perpendicular to and centered on the upright pole. The assembled cross could weigh more than one hundred kilograms. It was apparent to anyone watching the gruesome procession that Jesus was having difficulty carrying his cross. I figured the loss of blood, from the severe beatings the Jew had bore, were making the task almost impossible, and yet, he still pushed forward, a foot or two at a time.

The Legionnaire unit assigned to escort the condemned trio to "The Skull" grew impatient with Jesus' constant stumbling and they began to pummel him even harder with fists, feet, and whips. It was a vicious cycle. Jesus being weak from the abuse would stumble under the cross's weight, inflaming Legionnaire anger which resulted in further abuse, only to have Jesus stumble again. This cycle continued through the city.

Against my better judgment, I took Phillip up on his offer to attend a gathering of Jesus' followers.

CHAPTER NINE

THE NOONDAY SUN WAS a brilliant white and the air stifling as it sapped the energy out of me. Events from the previous night had not allowed me to sleep, so I was feeling extremely tired. I entertained the idea of turning back, but only briefly. I wasn't sure what to expect and I certainly had doubts about even going to this meeting. I had already been given my freedom and should have been far away from this madness, but something pulled at me to attend. Something inside of me compelled me to go.

Arriving at the two-story mud-brick structure, I carefully looked around for any sign of Legionnaires. Seeing none, I took a deep breath while making a final commitment. Covered with sweat, aching with fatigue, and trembling with anticipation, I pulled back the rugged, wool sheepskin covering the building's entry. As I stepped inside, my waning eyesight could not immediately adjust from the sunlight to the dark shadows of the musty room. As the shadows slowly formed into recognizable shapes, I squinted to make out the details of the room's interior. Reluctantly the shadows unveiled their secrets, and the sparsely furnished room came into view. A solitary ray of light penetrated a small opening in the room's wall. Pungent odors from soiled clothes and unwashed pots filled the air.

At first, I couldn't see or hear anything and wondered if I had entered the wrong building, or if some trap had been set for me and right now Legionnaires were secretly watching me. This last thought caused a hitch in my breath, in an insane attempt at concealing the sound of my breathing. In the quiet of the room, I could now make out the sound of my pounding heart, and there was a subtler sound of murmuring.

I remained quiet and concentrated on the sound and soon recognized voices. They were coming from the building's second floor. As I eased my way up the steps the voices became louder and the feeling of anxiousness came over me. When I stood before the gathered crowd, they appeared startled and grew quiet. It was Phillip who broke the silence, "Ah Barabbas, I am so glad you decided to come, welcome." Turning toward the crowd, Phillip walked towards a man who stood at the center. The man was of average height and weight, but his head seemed to be out of proportion in its immensity.

"Everyone, I'd like to introduce you to the man I was telling you about, Barabbas." Phillip introduced.

"We know who he is," came a voice from the group. "He got off from a death sentence and our savior got executed. Why did you bring him here?"

I was growing nervous and looked around for a route to make a hasty exit. Because the group had encircled me, I realized I would have to fight to escape. With my heart racing, I was about to dash out of there when another voice broke the silence.

"Welcome, Barabbas. Phillip has told us a great deal about you," said the man with the large head. "My name is Peter and since the death of Jesus, I am coordinating things the best I can while we attempt to figure out what's next."

I slowly made my way across the room toward Peter and grasped his extended hand. I noticed he had a pleasant warm smile on an otherwise rough exterior.

"I don't know why I'm here today. I suppose it's to try and get some answers as to what's going on," I stated. "As for Pilate granting me clemency, I don't know what that was all about and I certainly had no part in it other than being the recipient of good fortune. I am sorry your leader died, but . . . ."

"Oh, he's not dead!" Peter interrupted. "And it was neither fortune nor luck that . . . "

"What do you mean he's not dead? I saw him crucified!" I exclaimed, interrupting.

"Yes, he was crucified and taken down from the cross dead, but he has arisen and . . . "

"Wait . . . Hold on, what do you mean he has arisen?"

"Just that," A woman in the group offered. "His tomb is empty, the Lord has risen."

"You mean someone broke into the tomb and stole his body?" I inquired. "I know what the Romans are saying. They say some of you broke into the tomb when the posted guards weren't looking and stole his body."

"Barabbas, think for a minute. It took fifteen Legionnaires to roll away a very large stone in front of the tomb entrance before Jesus was placed in it." Peter explained. "How would fifteen or more of us be able to sneak up to the tomb and then quietly roll away the stone without being seen? Does that make any sense?"

"As much sense as you trying to tell me he has risen," I answered. "And what do you mean risen?"

"Just that Barabbas," Phillip stated. "Jesus has risen. He's alive!"

"Have you all gone crazy? Arisen? Alive?" I posed incredulously. "Dead men don't get up again."

"Nonetheless. Be that as it may, Mary," Phillip continued pointing to a very pretty, young Jewish woman. "Went to the tomb the first thing this morning, before the sun was up, and . . . well, why don't I let her tell you. Mary, would you? I know you're still shaken, but please, tell your story again."

"Oh sir," Mary began. "I know you will think me mad, but I assure you, I am telling the truth. This morning, after a night in which I could not sleep, I got up. After dressing I had the overwhelming urge to go to Jesus' tomb. I knew we were going to go later and prepare his body properly, but something in me made me go to the tomb. As I approached the burial ground, I could feel something different and yet wonderful had happened so I began to run. As I approached his tomb, I noticed the guards assigned to watch over his crypt were running about in a confused manner and yelling at one another like madmen.

"The large boulder used by the guards to seal the tomb was rolled away and a faint glow was coming from within. I slowly crept towards the opening and as I drew nearer, an intense feeling of peace came over me, as if everything wrong would now be right. As I got to the entrance, my heart was banging hard as I just knew, inside me, what I would find."

"What? What would you find?" I asked, my curiosity getting the better of me.

"What I saw was an empty tomb. The cloth we had used to wrap Jesus' body was still there, wrapped just as we had put them on his body, but his body was gone. You could see the wrappings had not been untied, nor had they been moved.

"I heard a rustling sound coming from behind me and quickly became certain I would be facing an inquiry from a Legionnaire. What I saw instead was two men, or at least I think they were men. They were very beautiful and they told me not to cry. I had begun crying because I was sure someone from the Legion had stolen Jesus' body and I wouldn't be able to prepare him."

"So what did these beautiful men say?" I anxiously asked.

"They told me not to cry that Jesus was not in the tomb but had risen just as he said he would and I must go and tell the rest of his followers. I quickly ran out of there and didn't stop running until I came here and told the others."

"When she got here." Peter began. "She told us the same story as you just heard and understandably, we too, could not believe her. Of course, some of us remembered Jesus telling us that he would return after he left us, but we didn't think he meant like this. We thought he meant he needed a little time away from everyone and would return, but this, this was . . . this was just so incredible. Anyway, some of us quickly ran to the tomb to see for ourselves and sure enough, the boulder had been rolled away, Legionnaires were searching the area and the tomb was empty."

"And you believe this story? All of you believe what? That someone has stolen Jesus' body or . . . ?" I inquired.

"No sir, not stolen," He countered. "Jesus has arisen and is alive again. He said . . . "

"Come on," I said laughing. "You believe he is roaming around somewhere amongst the living? You can't be serious!"

Watching their faces I could see they were indeed serious. They looked deadly serious and that worried me. I was determined to excuse myself from their imploring eyes and get out of town as fast as I could.

"Look, I am truly sorry for the loss of your leader and I don't know why the people asked for my release instead of his, but I really must be going. It won't be long before Pilate's men come looking for me and I want to be long gone before then."

I didn't wait to hear their response as I bolted for the doorway. No one attempted to impede my exit so I slowed down to a fast walk. Pushing back through the sheepskin entrance as I headed toward the road, I couldn't help looking behind me as an extremely bright flash of light emanated from within the building. It was so bright I would have believed it if someone had told me the sun had just exploded.

For several seconds my vision was impaired and I felt certain I was blind. As my sight gradually returned, I could see a pulsating light coming from behind the sheepskins that covered the doorway and upper floor windows. I was sure everyone as far away as Jericho would have seen the intense flash, including Legionnaires who were bound to come investigating, but as I turned to quickly leave the area, I was amazed to see the citizenry traveling along the street in front of the building as if nothing strange had just happened.

A stooped, ragged, and aged man shuffled reluctantly along the street pushing a cart loaded with various odds and ends. From the direction in which he was going and his slow pace, I realized he would have been directly in front of the building as I came out and the flash occurred. I had to find out what he saw.

Catching up to the old man, I grabbed his arm and swung him around. The fear in his eyes at my seizing him was evident and I was immediately sorry for having disturbed him.

"Sir, I don't mean to bother you and I certainly didn't mean to scare you." I offered.

"I didn't do nothin'."' The man volunteered. "It was just layin'" in the street. I saw no one around, so I figured nobody wanted it. I didn't . . . "

"Whoa. Hold on!" I interrupted. "I'm not going to hurt you and I don't care what you found."

"You're not going to report me to the Legion?" He asked in disbelief.

"No. Do I look like someone who works for the Legion?"

"Can't be sure these days. They say Pilate has spies everywhere and I'm too old to be sent to the dungeons, so Pilate would have me killed immediately."

"Well I'm not with the Legion and I owe no allegiance to Pilate," I said. "I was just wondering if when you walked past the front of that building there," I pointed. "Did you see anything odd? Anything out of the ordinary?"

"No sir, can't say I did? You said you just came out of there?" He asked me.

"Yes, why?"

"Well, if you just came out of there, then if anything odd happened, you would have seen it then, right?" He asked quizzically with a toothless grin.

I decided I would not get anywhere with the old man and had better get going, someone had to have seen a flash that bright and would now be on their way to see what had caused it.

"Sorry to have bothered you, sir," I stated and quickly walked away. *I could feel the old man watching me and no doubt wondering if I was crazy.*

As quickly as I could I got out of town and headed south to the town of Bethany. It was there that Lukoi, a former member of the rebellion had retired to. In one of our earlier raids against a Legion outpost, he had been thrust through the shoulder with a spear and no longer had use of his left arm. His injury had accomplished more than physical harm, he had grown increasingly fearful at any sudden noise or movement and feared he would be captured and tortured at any given moment.

CHAPTER NINE

Sensing Lukoi's fear and possible danger to the rebellion, Bab-bukia sent him home. Upon leaving our encampment, Lukoi was exceedingly joyful and invited all of us to his home if we ever made it his way.

CHAPTER TEN

SPOTTING A YOUNG BOY *along the road, I asked him if he knew where Lukoi lived and he indicated everyone knew where the crazy man lived and then gave me the directions to Lukoi's hut.*

Making my way toward the small opening of the solitary, diminutive mud hut I entered upon hearing humming from within. At first, I did not recognize the once mighty warrior, as he looked more tattered than an overused rag. And then I noticed his eyes. His eyes no longer reflected the fear and desperate loneliness of wondering when he might be discovered and killed. They were simply glazed with what I felt was the hopelessness that reaches far beyond poverty and hunger into the bottomless abyss of one who no longer lives but merely exists.

"Lukoi, how are you doing?" I asked, extending my hand.

The man I once knew I could depend on to watch my back during a fight just looked at my hand and then stared at my face as if he could not recognize me.

"It's me, Barabbas." I offered.

Recognition replaced doubt and a wide grin etched across his face. "Ah, Barabbas and how goes it with my good friend?"

"Well, now that I am out of Jerusalem." I stated.

"You were in Jerusalem?" Lukoi asked, surprised.

"Yes, I was in the dungeons just two days ago and…"

"Pilate's dungeons?" Lukoi asked, baffled.

"Yes, Pilate's dungeons. After you left the rebellion, we raided the town of Aenon and were quickly overrun. We lost many good men and women martyrs in the battle, and the rest of us were captured and sent to the dungeons. Many more were made spectacles for Pilate's macabre games and..."

"And how did you get out?" Lukoi suspiciously wondered. "No one who goes in ever comes out again."

"Good question, Lukoi. I am still trying to figure that out myself. You see, it was just before the Jewish Passover and while the dungeons were full, Pilate decided to honor a Jewish tradition by releasing one of the prisoners locked up." I explained.

"Oh yeah, I heard about that. Word has it that the Jews asked Pilate to release an insurgent instead of . . . hey wait a minute, you're not going . . . " Lukoi stammered.

"Yes Lukoi, it was I the Jews asked to release." I acknowledged. But I still don't know why.

Lukoi looked around nervously as if he expected someone to come and accost us. "Are you sure no one followed you here, or . . . or . . . sent you here?" He asked.

I understood his doubt and put in the same predicament, I too would have wondered about anyone who had been released from Pilate's dungeons.

"Don't worry old friend, no one knows I am here and I am no spy for the Legion. I hate them as much today as the day they killed my family. The only reason I am here is that I am trying to rest before I get as far away from Judea as I possibly can."

"Then you were in Jerusalem when Jesus was killed?" He asked me. His question startled me to know anyone outside of the city would be aware of a rebel's death.

"You know of Jesus then?" I asked.

"Oh yes, I've met him." Came the unexpected reply.

"You met him? How? Where?"

"If you remember, after we attacked that Roman outpost, I was severely injured and had lost the use of my left arm."

"Yes, I remember. That was the reason you left the rebellion and came here." I recounted.

"That's right. Anyway, as I made my way from Ephraim to come here, I saw a large gathering of people near a well in the center of a small dust-ridden town in the middle of nowhere." He began. "I was thirsty and hungry and wanted to see if I could work for some provisions. Seeing the gathering, I made my way toward them. As I drew closer I realized something compelling had to be happening because no one looked in my direction as I came up behind them. Working my way through the crowd, I was able to see a man who was holding their attention with some kind of speech. He was surrounded by what looked to be twelve bodyguards and he seemed to be speaking about peace and love to all men, even our enemies."

"When I asked some in the gathering who the man speaking was, they acted incredulous that I was not aware who Jesus was. Upon further questioning, I was informed he was some kind of great prophet, or to be precise, they said he was the savior spoken of in some ancient prophecy come to save the Jews and all of mankind."

"As I stood at the front of the assembly, I watched as Jesus put his hand on a young girl's deformed foot, and I swear I'm not making this up, the girl's foot was healed. It was just as good as if nothing had ever been wrong with it. She got up out of the basket her family had carried her in and ran up to Jesus and kissed his cheek. I couldn't believe it."

"And you saw this with your own eyes? I asked in amazement.

"Yes and not only did I see it with my own eyes, I somehow gathered up enough nerve to approach him myself, and let me tell you, as soon as I was in his presence I felt a peace come over me I have never felt before. As I drew within a couple of feet of him, he looked at me and smiled and I almost fell to my knees with feelings of guilt, instead, I found myself crying like a baby. He gently touched my shoulders and looked into my eyes and told me I was filled with a lot of grief and sin, and that I was to give up the fighting and go in peace. When he released me, I was astounded to find that my left arm was completely healed and I cried even more."

"I tell you Barabbas, I wanted to join him right then but it was like he could read my mind. He told me to go my way and to spread the word of love to all. Later I was told by some of the town's people that everywhere Jesus went, large groups of people spring up and openly rebel against the Romans with a mission of peace."

"Well, I for one can tell you it isn't much of a rebellion." I voiced.

"What? What do you mean it's not much of a rebellion?" Lukoi asked, disappointed.

According to what I've been told the twelve bodyguards you mentioned is the extent of the rebellion's army. Oh, excuse me, eleven, one of the twelve killed himself when Jesus was arrested."

"How do you know all this, Barabbas?"

"I heard it straight from Jesus' mouth. He was locked up in the dungeon at the same time as me."

"So you've met Jesus?"

"Not only did I meet him and speak with him, but it was I the Jews asked to be released instead of Jesus." I enlightened.

"You . . . Wait . . . You mean to tell me you're the rebel Pilate released to the Jews? You?"

"Yes, and I still don't understand it. How or why it happened. All I know is I am glad but don't get me wrong, I am extremely sorry he died in my place, but how can I not be happy?"

After saying it I felt extremely dirty and guilty and again wondered why I was feeling that way. I had long ago given up feelings of compassion towards others as a weakness that could get you killed, but somehow the thought of Jesus not only required me to have compassion but understanding as well.

"You know something?" Lukoi began. "Since word of the crucifixion filtered throughout the countryside, I've had the chance to speak with many Jews and most of them have these wild ideas about what this Savior or Messiah would or could do."

"The hope of this Messiah takes many forms with most looking for the perfect successor to King David, who will establish a Kingdom for the Jews and banish their enemies."

"Okay, so what did Jesus think about all this talk concerning his being this Messiah?" I asked.

"Well, you can well imagine that he wouldn't admit it in public. To do so would be to invite misunderstanding. Every Jew who heard the term would be thinking in terms of eventual rebellion against the Romans, and of a great day when a Jewish empire would replace Rome." Lukoi explained.

"Yeah, that may be true, but I understand he never really rejected the claim. Isn't that what ultimately led to his crucifixion?" I asked

"Indeed. He did not object to the mocking claim by Caiaphas, but he tried to explain how they had mistaken the claim. You have to realize Barabbas, one reason for Jesus' reluctance to be called Messiah before, was the idea it would be wrongly understood. He believed he was the Messiah, but not of the kind most people expected."

"If I might ask, how do you know so much about all of this? I inquired.

"After my miracle." Lukoi paused. Addressing my doubtful look he continued. "Yeah miracle, Barabbas. Remember, I couldn't use my arm until I looked in his eyes and he touched me."

"For many days after that, I walked around in a dazed state, not knowing what had happened. I'll tell you Barabbas, I didn't know who I was."

"Don't get me wrong, I knew I was Lukoi, but I didn't know who I truly was."

"And, so what, now you know?" I asked skeptically. "So you've had this great revelation of who you truly are, huh?"

"There is still much I don't know, but I know this, I too am now a follower of Jesus, and I no longer fear Pilate, Herod or Caesar himself." Lukoi said with an air of confidence.

"So how did all of this come about? I thought you said you left and wandered after your mira . . . hmm, um your healing."

"That's right, after my miracle, I did wonder about the countryside. But I'll tell you something, Barabbas, many in the crowd who followed Jesus, knew the effect he could have and sent a man to find me, and answer my questions."

"It seems one of them, Nekodiz is his name, had walked with Jesus as one of the seventy selected by Jesus to assist the disciples in spreading his teachings. I think you called them bodyguards."

"After Jesus was executed his disciples fled as a decree went out across the land to arrest all followers of the rebel Jesus and that meant sure death, so all of the disciples and fringe followers fled. Nekodiz came here to hide."

"The people of Bethany, having committed to serve Jesus, hid Nekodiz until the Legionnaires looking for him passed through. Over the days that followed, he told us the stories of Jesus."

"And where did this Nekodiz go? I would imagine by now he's long gone, but if you could tell me in which direction he went, perhaps I could catch up to him." I stated.

"If you were to catch up with him, what would you do?" Lukoi asked protectively.

"I would sit down with him and ask many questions. Having been in Jesus' presence, something changed inside me and I want to know how and why." I explained.

Apparently satisfied I meant no harm, Lukoi said. "In that case, you can find him living at the home of Jesse on the edge of town just down the road."

Thanking Lukoi for his help, I left to find Nekodiz. A strange exhilaration came over me. If I had been asked I wouldn't have been able to explain the feeling, all I know is I felt happy and alive, and better than I had felt in many years.

CHAPTER ELEVEN

FINDING THE HOME OF Jesse, I called out to the occupants and was met at the doorway by a heavily built Jewish man who angrily asked for my name and what I wanted.

"My name is Barabbas," I said, introducing myself while extending a hand. "I come from the town of Nain and I was told I could find Nekodiz here."

He paused while rubbing gnarly-looking fingers through a scruffy beard as he assessed my response.

"And why do you want to find Nekodiz? Does he know you?" Came his reply.

"No, no he doesn't know me, but I was speaking to a good friend down the road,

you may know him, Lukoi, anyway he said I might be able to find Nekodiz here and get some of my questions answered." I clarified.

"And what sort of questions might they be?"

"I have many questions concerning a Jewish man the Romans crucified named Jesus and was told Nekodiz walked with him."

"And supposing that were true, what does that have to do with you? The Romans would like to know where Nekodiz is as well. I am sure you are aware Pilate and Herod have decreed anyone who knew Jesus or follows his teachings should be arrested." This Jew revealed.

"Yes, I am aware of that," I confirmed. "I also realize you have no reason to trust me and I wouldn't blame you if you don't, but I'll confide in you a fact that is detrimental to my safety as well. As I earlier introduced myself, I am Barabbas and what you may not be aware of, I am the man Pilate released during the Passover celebration instead of Jesus. You can check around and you will see that I too am very much wanted by the Legionnaires."

The Jew stared hard at me for what seemed a long time before he finally stated, "I know all about you and your freedom Barabbas, and I don't think you are a threat. I am he you have come to see. I am Nekodiz. What are your questions?"

"While I have many questions concerning the man who was responsible for saving my life, I guess the first question would be, why did his people turn on him?"

"A very good question Barabbas." Nekodiz began. "And one I am not completely sure I can answer but I will try."

"During the celebration week of Passover, as you are no doubt aware, several hundred thousand Jews had assembled in Jerusalem, and I'll be honest, at first I was scared. I couldn't believe so many people knew of Jesus and they swarmed us. They spread clothes and tree branches across the road to show adoration."

"Usually Jesus recoiled from displays of fanaticism, but this time he let them yell. It looked for all the world as if a King had arrived in force to claim his throne."

"So how did Jesus feel about all the attention given him?" I wanted to know.

"We had asked him that same question and Jesus explained that his feelings were mixed because he knew how easily a crowd could turn, and he was right. It made no sense. With such a throng throwing themselves at his feet one week, how did Jesus get arrested and killed the next?"

"We were all determined to be very cautious about what we said after watching a Roman officer arrive to check on the crowd and disturbance. I can only imagine what that Roman must have thought when he saw the forlorn looking figure riding on the back of a donkey with a borrowed tunic draped across it's back."

"Jesus actually knew and warned us that things would quickly take a turn for the worse."

"But I am confused," I confessed. "The people who brought charges against him were of the same faith, surely they should have been more merciful."

"Ah yes, you would think so but try to understand, when Jesus stood before Pilate, those who did oppose and accuse him were not godless people but as you pointed out, religious leaders, the High Priest . . . "

"Caiaphas?" I interjected.

"That's right. Caiaphas together with the other chief priests and the whole Sanhedrin had declared Jesus was worthy of death. They brought him to Pilate to solidify their judgment so that Jesus might be executed."

"But you have to realize this was not a sudden development. The trial before Pilate was the climax of opposition to Jesus which had grown through his ministry."

"But why were the leaders so opposed to him?" I questioned.

"Well, Jesus was a very remarkable, charismatic person. Consider, those of us who followed him gave up everything we had to be with him. There was something about that . . . that just reached into you and could seemingly feel you."

"Yeah! Yeah, that's it!" I explained with excitement. "I felt the same thing just looking into his eyes. Even though he had been beaten and whipped, his eyes still commanded."

"And that's how everyone who met Jesus felt. After his teaching began, we went with him to Nazareth where he had been brought up. In the temples, he read from the teachings of the prophet Isaiah and spoke of the promise of the Messiah's coming being then and there fulfilled."

"At first congregations were amazed but they soon became hostile. They completely failed to recognize Jesus as a prophet. He reminded them that when the prophets had met similar unbelief they had worked their wonders among heathens, implying the teachings would go to the Gentiles. Because he made such a suggestion the angry crowd sought to throw Jesus over a cliff. The high priests had taught them God would accept only their kind."

"And when all of these things were going on, where were you and his other followers?" I asked incredulously at what I was hearing.

"During those times when he was going to speak in a temple, Jesus would send us out in advance to spread his teachings," Nekodiz answered contemplatively."

"Like he knew trouble was coming and he wanted to spare you all?" I asked.

"I hadn't thought of that but you may be right. Jesus was always looking out for everyone else's welfare and if he felt there would be trouble he would have wanted to protect us."

"But Barabbas, friend. Can I call you a friend?" Nekodiz asked.

"I wish you would, I would be honored to be called your friend."

"Then my friend, the day grows old and we have not eaten. Mariah, Jesse's wife is a good cook and I am sure she will be pleased to serve one more."

That night while getting to know my new friends, I enjoyed a succulent meal of lamb, leeks, dates, figs, a fine bread made of millet, and a light refreshing gourd of wine.

After the meal, I grew tired as events from the day took their toll. I was preparing to go outside and find a comfortable place to sleep when Jesse indicated I would do no such thing.

"We have enough room here for you. There is clean straw over in the corner and you can make a bed anywhere you choose. Besides, if the Romans were to ride by as you slept, well . . . "

After bidding everyone a good sleep, I turned to make a bed when Nekodiz said, "Friend, sleep well. There will be time to talk in the morning and I must hear how you came to be in the predicament you were in, and how you knew Jesus."

Most of the next morning I spent explaining to Nekodiz, Mariah, and Jesse the facts surrounding my knowing Jesus, as well as how and why I had joined the rebellion. They all understood the radical change that had overtaken me after the death of my family and seemed not to judge my killing of the Legionnaire.

"So now what, Barabbas?" Nekodiz asked. "Where will you go? What will you do? You know the Romans will never give up looking for you. If it had been a Jew, Samaritan, or just about anyone else they might forget about you, but you took the life of a Roman citizen and they will never stop looking for you."

"Yes, I am well aware of that but I made a choice, sworn over the graves of Rebekah and Dodavah, and I will never stop fighting the Romans. With Pilate's decree, my death is imminent, and you know what? I don't care."

"You could stay here with us in Bethany." Jesse offered.

"Thank you, my friend. If it were under any other condition I would accept but to stay here would only put you all in jeopardy as well. Besides, I have some unfinished business in Jerusalem."

"Jerusalem?" Nekodiz questioned. "Barabbas, are you crazy? What could you possibly have to do in Jerusalem? Every Legionnaire on both sides of the Jordan is out looking for you and you're just going to saunter into their stronghold and do what? What could you possibly hope to accomplish there except get yourself killed?"

"I'm not sure Nekodiz, all I know is my heart is telling me I must get back to Jerusalem. Once I get there I'll try to figure why I'm there." I enlightened.

Packing some provisions offered by Mariah and Jesse, I said my goodbyes and headed back toward Jerusalem. Back to what fate I wasn't sure.

CHAPTER TWELVE

LOOKING UP AT JESUS' *face now, I realized I was too late to do anything that could have saved him. His fate had been decided by Pilate and according to Jesus, by prophecies long ago. Even if I had the rebellion's full complement behind me, it would not have been enough or made a difference and would only serve to get many men and women killed.*

Why had I come? What compelled me to make such a dangerous journey back to the place of so much grief? I suppose I could have said it was his eyes and the feeling I had of remorse, but remorse for what? What had I done to Jesus? Could I, in some way, be responsible for his death because the Jews had selected me to live? Could I have refused to be freed and if such lunacy were possible, then what? I consoled myself with the understanding that no matter what I did or said, the Romans were going to put Jesus to death.

As I now looked up at Jesus hanging on that horrid cross I couldn't help but wonder exactly what it was he had done to deserve this. The two common thieves hanging next to him understood what the law said and could not argue their punishment but Jesus, all he had done, whether delusional or not, was a claim to be the Son of God and could provide a better life for all who believed him. Surely that was not a reason to put him to death.

Off a short distance from his cross, several Legionnaires were loudly involved in a gambling game and randomly took turns screaming insults up at the condemned men, with the harshest insults reserved for Jesus. It was at that moment a very strange thing occurred, Jesus looked down upon his tormentors and cried out to no one I could see, saying something like "forgive them, it's not their fault." I couldn't be sure exactly what he said because his voice was being drowned out by the ever-increasing insults of the soldiers.

I looked over the ever-growing crowd and was surprised to find these were not the hecklers who had verbally assaulted Jesus as he struggled through the towns streets, these people were crying and screaming that Jesus was their Lord and Savior.

At the fringe of the gathering, I spotted a man I had only just seen earlier yet something inside told me I needed to speak with him. Making my way through the crowd I was standing beside Simon the Cyrenian who had helped carry Jesus' cross. Cautiously I inched closer and must have caught him off guard as he jumped as if shocked.

"Simon?" I asked. "I'm sorry to have frightened you. I saw you and wanted to talk to you."

His countenance was a mixture of fear and sadness as he asked me, "Who are you and what do you want with me? If you are a Legionnaire I have done nothing wrong. I carried his cross as you commanded but that is all."

"Simon, I'm not with the Legion and I am not a Roman spy. I am just trying to get some answers and I thought you might be able to help."

"Are you a follower of Christ, then?" He asked.

"Ah, well . . . No . . . No, I'm not, but I'd like to learn more about the man over there on the cross." I stammered.

"You mean Jesus. His name is Jesus, not just some man on the cross over there." Simon answered tersely.

"Yes, Jesus. I'm sorry for my callousness. I want to learn more about him. I've heard so much about him and..."

"Yeah, well I'm not the one you should be asking. I don't know much about him only that I now know he is the Son of God, the living Savior and they are putting him to death. I can't help you sorry."

Just like that Simon turned and walked away in the direction of the cross. It seemed as if by a silent signal only his followers could hear, the whole crowd moved closer to the crosses.

Suddenly the sky began to darken as massive clouds that weren't there a minute earlier, rumbled in. The day had begun under blue skies with not a cloud in sight and now it had darkened with such intensity that it appeared the hours had shifted and it was now night.

In the distance, working their way towards us, a line of lightning sizzled and crackled setting many trees and huts on fire and then the horrific began. The earth began shaking and people fell after losing their balance. Panic ensued as the crowd began running, not sure where to run to, they began running into each other.

Terrible rumblings like the earth being split in two preceded massive openings in the ground that swallowed up those standing too close. I was about to run for cover when I looked up at the face of Jesus and saw that his eyes were closed. They looked like they had finally found peace and that the suffering had at last finished. It was then that I noted he was bleeding from his side and not breathing.

Screaming from a great distance away announced that the temple had been destroyed and people were proclaiming the end of the earth had arrived. I learned later the curtain to the entrance of an area the priests called the "Holy of Holies" had ripped open while splintering wood crashed on the floor below.

A solitary Legionnaire stood transfixed at the foot of Jesus' cross as if glued to the spot. I stepped closer and heard him state breathlessly something about Jesus being who he said he was, and then he too ran off.

I stood gazing up a bit longer and then something tore at my heart and I found myself crying. My eyes welled with tears and through them I could see the beauty that was the man and I found myself crying out like so many others who stood nearby.

As terror ensued upon those who had harassed Jesus during his life, the very earth seemed to swallow them up now upon his death, and yet I was able to walk away without any fear for my life. His life had been traded for mine and I wasn't being tormented. I didn't know what it meant but I was determined to find out.

Instantly the great and foreboding cloud that had gathered around Golgotha disappeared. I was later to learn this was the first time Passover had been spent in chaos. Terrified priests attempted to find some way to cover over the entrance into the Holy of Holies and yelling to the panicked crowd they should not be looking at it.

I walked down the hill glancing back once to see the silhouettes of three crosses and began crying again. Walking the streets of Jerusalem I had no idea where I was going as I was in a dazed state, but my condition quickly changed when two Roman guards pointed at me and began crossing the street in my direction. I turned down a side street and picked up my pace hoping to elude them before they too turned down the street. It was to no avail as they quickly closed the distance and called out to me.

"You, halt! You there, halt now or feel Roman punishment." One of the Legionnaires yelled.

I knew I was doomed but I wasn't about to just give up, to do so was certain death because of the warrant Pilate had issued for me, so I broke into an all-out run. Not knowing the streets I ran aimlessly up one and down another, always hearing their footsteps behind me. They neither grew louder or fainter but stayed steady and that gave me a little room for hope. I made the mistake of turning down a street with no exit and quickly found it neither had any breaches in the buildings that lined it into which I could escape.

Trapped like a cornered animal I could do nothing but wait for the soldiers to turn onto the street I now stood. With the sound of my heart beating in my ears, I waited what seemed like hours for the Legionnaires to come but they never turned down the street. Slowly I began to make my way back toward the street's entryway expecting at any minute to see those who had chased me glowering in my direction.

At the entrance to the street, I looked about and didn't see the Romans. Standing across the way was a child of about twelve years who was staring at me.

"Mister?" the child called out. "Are you looking for the soldiers?"

"Did you see where they went, son?" I asked hopefully.

"Yeah, they were following you until you turned down that street, and then they both were grabbing at their eyes like they were blind. They were stumbling about screaming that they couldn't see. They staggered down that way and didn't come back."

I couldn't believe it, they were so close to catching me and something blinds them? What was going on? I could feel a smile growing on my face.

I made my way back through side streets to the building I had last seen Phillip and made my way up the dusty stairs. Voices could be heard and they sounded like people singing. At the top of the stairs, I could see close to a hundred people, both men, and women, and they were joyously singing, smiling, and clapping their hands.

Phillip looked in my direction and beckoned me to come to join them but I remained where I was and waited for them to stop. While the joyous occasion did not stop, Phillip made his way over to me.

"Barabbas, it's so good to see you again, how are you, my friend?"

"I am better now. I was almost captured by a couple of Legionnaires on my way here, but I seemed to have lost them. What's going on? Why all the excitement?" I inquired.

"This has been going on almost continually since you left," Phillip explained.

"Because I left?" I asked dumbfounded.

"No, Barabbas." Phillip laughed. "Not because you left, but what took place just after you left."

"And what was that?"

"I don't know if you'll understand what I am about to say, but believe me when I say it confirms for us who Jesus was . . . excuse me . . . who Jesus is."

"After you left the room we began to discuss everything including your being here. I probably don't need to tell you some in the group didn't feel comfortable with you being in our midst, they felt you would bring more trouble to everyone since a separate decree went out from the governor to have you arrested at all cost. It seems Pilate was embarrassed throughout the Roman Empire when others learned that the Jews had forced him to release an enemy of Caesar. To ensure you are captured, Pilate with Herods blessing has promised three oxen, a donkey, and two shekels to anyone who turns you in, as well as freedom to any slave. So you may well understand everyone's nervousness."

"I . . . I . . . had no idea how desperately they wanted me recaptured. So what do I do now?" I asked, perplexed.

"Nothing," Phillip said smiling. "As I said a little while ago after you left something happened that changed everything for us and confirmed who Jesus is."

"That's right, you did say that. So what happened and why do you insist that Jesus is still with us?" I wanted to know.

"Because he is. After he was crucified Jesus was taken down and temporarily put into a tomb and his body covered with some prepared cloth, as is our custom."

"I am well aware of that custom, but you said temporarily, why wasn't his body permanently prepared?"

"If you understand our customs, then you know by our laws we are not permitted to work on the Sabbath . . . "

"That's right, I do know that, so?"

"Well, Jesus was taken down just before dusk and the Sabbath was to begin, so we had just enough time to have him put into the tomb and the women vowed to go back in the morning to finish preparing his body for burial. The next morning Mary got up early and went to begin the process and came flying back here about two hours later crying and laughing that Jesus was gone, that his body was not in the tomb."

"We thought she was experiencing severe grief and was for the time being out of her mind because we had watched an entire unit of Legionnaires as they rolled a large boulder into place to block the entrance. Short of the entire unit being in on a conspiracy, someone would have had to see the boulder being moved."

"The funny thing is, the Legion Commander himself threatened every man in the unit with execution if they did not tell him where Jesus' body was. He was so incensed, he took a member of the unit and had a spear thrust through him as an example. When other members of the unit began to cry and babble about not knowing anything, the Commander stormed out of the area to make a report to Pilate."

"So where is Jesus' body then? Did someone from your people hide his body? I asked.

"That's what I've been trying to tell you, Jesus' body was not there because he has risen . . . "

"Oh come on Phillip, you can't believe that Jesus somehow lived through the crucifixion and then was taken down from the cross without anyone knowing he was still living. And then he's put into a tomb with a boulder weighing close to a thousand kilograms blocking the opening and he somehow what, rolls the boulder away?"

"I know how it sounds and we didn't believe it either until the day you came and wanted us to answer some of your questions. Remember that day?" Phillip asked.

"Oh yes, I remember. After I left and exited the building an intense light flooded the entrance and even though it was daytime, flashed into the street. What was that? I solicited.

"I'm getting to that and more. Before you arrived, as I said, Mary rushed in telling us that he was gone, you may well understand how we felt. Our Lord and Savior had been removed from his grave and we weren't sure if we would get the chance to prepare his body."

"Two of us immediately ran to the tomb to see for ourselves and just as Mary had said, the tomb was empty and no one, including the soldiers seemed to know what happened or where his body was."

"Mary told us that two men in white clothes and glowing as if the sun was behind them spoke to her telling her that Jesus was not there because he had risen as he had said he would many times."

"We had heard him say things like that in the past, but we figured he was speaking in riddles again. Jesus was always speaking in riddles to see if we understood what he was saying."

"Well, Thomas wasn't having any of Mary's story. He thought she had gone crazy and said we should all calm down and not start panicking that maybe Joseph, the rich man from Arimathaea, who had lent us his tomb to put Jesus in, had moved him for some reason. This was logical so we went to Joseph and asked him. Imagine the look he had when we explained Jesus' body was missing.

"Returning here, we all gathered to discuss what could have happened and the debate grew very lively when all of a sudden, the whole room filled with a blinding light. It was so bright it actually hurt my head and temporarily blinded us all."

"That must have been the light I saw out on the street," I exclaimed excitedly. "The way and time you described it, there could be no other explanation."

Phillip nodded in agreement.

"So what was it, what was that intense light?" I asked.

"Jesus." Came the response.

"Jesus? What do you mean, Jesus?" I asked in disbelief.

"After you left us Barabbas, we got involved in a pretty lively debate concerning the possible whereabouts of Jesus' body. This led to further discussions about Mary's encounter with two men and finally, remembering Jesus' own words."

"Jesus' own words? You mean he mentioned his body would be moved after he was entombed?" I asked.

"No, not that his body would be moved, but that he would be resurrected and would be with us again."

"Jesus said that? He said he would be resurrected or rise again?"

"Oh yes, he said it, many times, and that is what happened. As I was saying, after you left and Mary came back with the news that his body was no longer in the tomb, some of us remembered his words, but just like you, we found it so incredible that we felt it impossible. The one with the most doubt was Thomas, he felt Jesus was dead and that was that."

"As we began to pray for one another's safety, the room began to fill with a growing light. It didn't seem to come from anyplace, in particular, it just was."

"How can something just be? It had to have a beginning and end, where and when did it begin?" I asked.

"That's just it, it didn't begin anywhere or end, it just was. The light gradually grew in intensity until the entire room was filled with a light so bright we were forced to cover our eyes and yet, there was no pain."

"Just as quickly as the light filled the room it ended. We were all left stunned and began to ask each other what it was and what happened."

"As we looked around at each other, it was then that we noticed a beautiful stranger had entered our midst. We were in awe at his presence and then he spoke."

"What did he say?" I asked.

"He just spread his hands out before us and said Peace be to you." Phillip stated. Tears had begun to stream down his cheeks.

"As he spread his arms, we could all see the holes in his hands where the Romans had driven the spikes, and I know my eyes traveled to his feet and I could see the piercing of his ankles and I for one, at that point knew it was indeed Jesus, others were not sure.

"Thomas stated that until he could put his finger into the wounds he would not believe it was he. You see Thomas had seen many charlatans perform tricks and even the faking of a wound could be accomplished. He knew it would be impossible to fake an open wound, so he asked to feel the wound."

"So, did Jesus let him feel the wounds?" I asked.

"Oh yes, yes he did and instantly Thomas fell to his knees and proclaimed that it was, in fact, Jesus himself that had returned."

"Okay, so I am to believe that Jesus was crucified, died, and then arose from the dead? That's what you believe? I mean do you realize how that sounds?"

"Oh, I realize exactly how it sounds and if I hadn't seen it for myself and someone told me I would think they were crazy. Look, even though it sounds insane I and the other eleven aren't the only ones to witness it. There was . . . "

"Yes I know, Mary saw the empty tomb..."

"That's right, but not just her. Two of our group were walking from Bethany to get here, they were late for the Passover, and anyway, they had already received word about Jesus' crucifixion and were discussing it as they continued their travel. As they were walking a stranger fell in beside them and engaged them in conversation. They said they were expressing their sadness at the death of Jesus when the stranger revealed that it was he, Jesus, that walked with them. He also showed them the nail wounds and then he disappeared. They ran all the way here to let us know."

"Barabbas, there have been well over five hundred of us who have now seen him and know he is alive."

"Yeah, five hundred of his followers, and you all want to believe it and do believe it, but how? How is that even possible?" I asked.

"I know what you're saying and I don't blame you for how you feel, but you should try to understand this, with the decree from Caesar to have all of Jesus' followers taken into custody and knowing what the result would be, do you honestly think anyone would openly admit to being one of his followers?"

"I wouldn't think so, but…"

"But nothing, it would be purely insane to admit to even knowing Jesus at this time. Yet, each one of us is ready and have already proclaimed to not only know him but have accepted him as our Lord and Savior as well."

I was stunned and couldn't speak. Staring into his eyes I could see Phillip was speaking with a strange conviction that he was willing to die now if it was necessary. I was certain it was going to be necessary and I had no intent on dying for this cause. I felt my chances were better if I got away from these people as quickly as I could.

"Phillip, I am sure you believe all of this, but…" I began.

"I know, you sympathize with us, but you don't want to be a part of it?"

"I am sorry, but it's not my battle. You all have one heck of a fight on your hands and I know Pilate, Herod, and Caesar himself will not rest until all of you are destroyed. As for me, Pilate has vowed to have me recaptured so I too know what will be awaiting me."

"But where will you go, Barabbas, back to your old rebellion friends, those that haven't been caught yet?"

"No, that's exactly what I won't do. I don't have a plan but I know that I have to get as far away from Judea as I can. Maybe I'll make my way to Greece. I've heard they're pretty understanding people and don't bow down to Rome. Maybe I can hide out there and live life to old age." I speculated hopefully.

"Barabbas, we grow stronger every day and you would be a good candidate to spread his words." Phillip offered.

"No, I don't think so. You see, I can't see sitting around and waiting on my enemy to come and grab me as I go from house to house spouting off about a risen dead man. . . . I'm sorry, I shouldn't have said that," I stated contritely. I had seen a look of pain cross his face. "I guess it's all the frustration from the times we live in. That's also a good reason for me to be going, I'm on edge and wouldn't be very good at talking to others about Jesus. Besides, I don't know enough about him to speak to others anyway, but thanks for the offer."

"Well Barabbas, it seems you have made up your mind. We all wish you well in your travels and pray you to find whatever it is you are looking for." Phillip presented. "You're welcome here anytime."

"Thank you my friend and I hope all of you find what it is you are looking for."

"Oh, we already have but thank you anyway."

I made my way out of the room and quickly found a route that took me out of Jerusalem. I intended to make my way to Joppa, a bustling town known for its many fish vendors that sat next to the Mediterranean Sea. I was sure it was there that I would be able to find a vessel to Greece and freedom.

Chapter Thirteen

I grew tired. Walking what should have been a seemingly effort-less thirty-eight-kilometer journey had effectively become an eleven-kilometer quandary and I wasn't even close to my destination yet. It seemed Legionnaires were everywhere and while I had no way of knowing if they were looking for me, I could not take the chance. This forced me to take a very circuitous route.

Looking in the distance I could make out first one, then another, and finally several lights against the nighttime blackness. Carefully I walked toward the lights until I could see they were coming from a city.

At the edge of the now very alive city, I found a young shepherd boy attending his flock. I found myself transfixed by his movements. He reminded me so much of Dodavah and I couldn't help but feel the tears welling up in my eyes. Composing myself, I made my way to him and was taken aback when he quickly turned in my direction, a scowl on his face, and staff raised menacingly. Slowly his counte-nance changed to a smile that engulfed his entire face.

"I'm sorry mister, you scared me. With so many Romans in the area, I didn't want to lose any of the herd." The boy apologized.

"It's alright son, I understand. Look, I am new here and won-dered what town that might be?" I asked pointing in the distance.

"Oh that's Lydda and you're just in time for a week-long feast." Came his excited reply.

"Really? And what feast would that be?"

"You are new around here. Why is it the feast in celebration of the Roman's defeat in Jerusalem."

"Defeat? What defeat?" I asked. *I was beside myself with excitement. Could it be in the short few days it had taken me to walk here, an uprising had changed the tide in a portion of Judea. The Romans were defeated? By who . . . where?*

"Not in battle," the boy laughed. "There is no match for them in military might."

"Then what are you talking about?" I asked, a bit agitated.

"The Romans were defeated because they wanted so badly to kill Jesus of Nazareth and he has risen!" The boy exclaimed excitedly.

This was unbelievable, even out here in the middle of nowhere; the insanity of a risen dead man had taken hold. What could it mean?

"You said the Romans were defeated, can you tell me if there are any of them in Lydda?"

"No sir, I wouldn't think so. They fled out of here early, as soon as they heard about some trouble in Jerusalem. They had orders to join the others to put down any possible revolt." The boy explained.

"And would you know if Lydda is on the way to Joppa? I asked.

"Yes sir. You are going in the right direction. So you're going to Joppa?"

"Yes, I am." I answered.

"Well it's pretty dark out and the beasts of the night are all about. You might want to spend the night in town."

"That's some good advice, can you make a suggestion on a decent place to stay, get a meal and perhaps obtain provisions for a long journey?" I asked expectantly.

"You can get all of those things at Hiram's shop. Everyone knows him. He gets a little cranky, but he helps everyone and if he doesn't have what you're looking for, he usually knows where it can be found."

"Where can I find this Hiram?" I asked.

"That's easy too. He has the largest fish shop in Lydda and his tent is the most colorful. It has every color of the rainbow on it. It sits on the main road into and out of town, you can't miss it."

"Thank you very much, son. What is your name anyway?" I inquired.

"My name is Josiah the shepherd boy. Everyone in town knows me."

"Well thank you, Josiah, you have been a great help."

I continued down the trail that led into town, not sure what I would find there but with the strong conviction that I must be there.

Entering Lydda was like nothing I had ever seen before, people were everywhere. The flicker of candlelight seemed to illuminate from every open door and window, and I found myself wondering how possible it was for one of the buildings to go up in flames with no one to attend the candles. I was certain every man, woman, and child that were counted as citizens of Lydda was now on the town's streets joining in an endless stream of revelry.

As I jostled my way through the sea of humanity I made my way to a fish vendor's tent that closely resembled the shepherd boy's description. An equally colorful, yet very stooped man was arranging a fish display as I came up behind him.

"I am looking for . . . " I began.

The stooped man whirled about faster than I could have imagined. In his hand, he held a knife used for filleting fish. It looked very pointed, sharp, and menacing.

"Who are you and what are you doing sneaking up behind me?" The vendor asked.

His eyes seemed to sparkle with excitement at the thought of a confrontation. It was easy to see by his rough exterior he had seen his share of fights.

"I'm sorry if I scared you. I was not trying to sneak up behind you. My name is Barabbas, from the town of Nain, I'm..."

"Nain, huh? I was in Nain once, a grimy little town. Not very likable people I recall."

"It's only because the Romans have come through so many times and done so much harm that no one knows which stranger is a spy," I explained.

"Hmmmph." The vendor snorted.

My explanation settled his anxiety a bit because he laid the knife down.

"What did you say your name was again?" He asked.

"Barabbas. I am looking for a vendor by the name of Hiram. I was told I could find him at a tent just like this one."

"Well, this is the only tent like it in all of Judea." The man spoke proudly. "What do you want with Hiram?"

"Then you know him?"

"I know him, but you don't so before I tell you where you can find him, you tell me why you want him."

"Okay. A shepherd boy on the outskirts of town named Josiah told me a Hiram might be able to tell me where I can get something to eat, a place to sleep, provisions for a journey, and perhaps provide me with directions for the safest route to Joppa."

"Joppa? Now there's a wonderful city. Too big for me though. You see all these fish?" He asked, spreading his arms to indicate the many tables filled with all kinds of fish. "These all came from Joppa. I get to fish there every week from the coast. Of all the vendors I have the best supply of fish." He said bragging. Sounding more confident now he said, "I am Hiram. Let's go inside and see if I can help you."

Hiram's home was a very small but well-kept hut that his vendor's tent was attached to on the outside. I was surprised at the overall neatness when comparing it to the owner.

"So, you're going to Joppa, huh? So, how can I help you?"

"I was told you might be able to sell me some provisions for the trip to Joppa and on to Greece," I explained.

"Greece? You're going to Greece? What in heaven for? They're evil people, what with all forms of debauchery. They eat their own young, they do." Hiram stated emphatically.

"How do you know that? Ever been there?"

"To Greece?"

"Yes, to Greece. Ever been there?"

"Well, ah, no can't say I have. But I've heard all the stories the fishermen tell and it sounds like an evil place." He stated with a disgusted look.

"I'll just have to take my chances." I volunteered. "Can you help me with provisions?

Hiram seemed to amble aimlessly from one side of his home to the other, occasionally disappearing into a work area out back as he meticulously laid out items he felt I would need on my journey. Then he brought out an item that caught my attention and breath.

"Hiram, where did you get that?"

"What, this old spade-like thing?"

"It's not a spade, it's a goad. Where did you get it?" I asked.

"A goad? What in the world is a goad?" Hiram asked, perplexed.

"The pointed end there is used to direct oxen and the other end is used to plow.

"How'd you know that?" Hiram asked.

"Let me see that for a minute," I instructed, taking it from his hand.

Looking closely at the instrument, I was barely able to see the scratches but they were there. I pointed them out to Hiram.

"You see these marks on the handle?" I questioned pointing to the goad.

Hiram leaned close and squinted to see the marks I had indicated. "Yeah, I see something scratched on there. What is it?" He asked.

"Those are my marks. I made that goad about five years ago and put my mark on it like I did all of my tools. Where did you get this?"

"I suppose I could ask you the same thing. If it's yours as you say, what am I doing with it?" Hiram concurred.

"Okay listen, I don't have a lot of time so I'm going to take a chance and tell you a story and hope my tale is safe with you."

For the next hour, I explained to Hiram about Rebekah, Dodavah, the rebellion, my capture, and release from Pilate's dungeon.

Throughout the account, Hiram remained very quiet as if in deep thought. I concluded with why I was going to Greece.

"So you're going to Greece to escape the Romans then?"

"Yes, that's about right." I answered.

"Funny, I would have thought it was to hunt down the Roman responsible for killing your family." Hiram offered.

"What are you talking about, Hiram?"

"Well, you said this goad thing is yours right?"

"Yeah, so?"

"So, I got it from a Roman. Came in about three days ago saying he needed to buy some fish. Instead of paying with money, said he had something he was willing to trade. He produces this thing and while I didn't know what it was, it looked like it could be useful for something, so I traded him some fish for it."

"A Roman Legionnaire came here with that?" I asked excitedly.

"Yeah, he was part of the unit that left for Jerusalem."

My heart sank. I could not go back to Jerusalem without taking the risk of being captured and yet, the urge for revenge tugged at me all the more.

"So they're headed back to Jerusalem then?"

"No, the unit is, but the Roman who traded this thing is headed in the same direction you are. Said he was headed for Joppa."

Now my heart began to pound mightily in my chest and my breathing became very rapid. "Why was he headed to Joppa and his unit back to Jerusalem?" I asked.

"Said his Commander put him in charge of buying large quantities of fish for their outpost in Bethany. More fish than I have here, so he was going to purchase a lot more fish to be dried and delivered to their outpost."

"You said he came through here three days ago?"

"That's right, he left with four other Romans."

"And perchance, do you have a name and rank for this Roman?

"He was just a regular Legionnaire. Don't think he carried any rank but I did hear one of the others call him Gaucius."

"Gaucius, huh? Now I have to figure out how to catch him since he has a three-day head start."

"Well Barabbas, you're in luck. You see, the Romans are headed straight for Joppa and the road is long, but I know a way through a mountain pass that can get you there a day before them." I was encouraged.

The excitement was growing inside me, as was the renewed anger for the loss of my family.

"Okay Hiram, how do I catch up with them?"

"Oh no, not like that. You would never be able to find the pass by yourself. No, I'll have to show you."

"What do you mean you'll have to show me?

"Just that. I have to buy more fish anyway, so I might as well tag along with you. Besides, the company will be good." Hiram explained.

"Now wait a minute, I can't be responsible for you! I exclaimed.

"Responsible for me?" Hiram laughed. "I'm the one showing you through the mountain pass, besides I have no interest in confronting the Romans. No, I'm just guiding you through the pass to Joppa, then you're on your own."

"Okay, well since you put it like that, how soon can we get started?" I asked, smiling.

Hiram was turning out to be a pretty good fellow and I would certainly enjoy his companionship during the journey. He would help to keep my mind from being overtaken with vengeful thoughts.

The journey through the mountain pass was fairly easy compared to other mountainous journeys I had taken in the past. I would suppose it had a great deal to do with the guiding Hiram accomplished. He was a more than adequate and fast hiker and our elapsed time through the mountain was less than two days.

Chapter Fourteen

As we came down the mountain, Joppa could be seen in the distance, but it was the scene below us on the trail to Joppa that caught my attention. A small group of horsemen had made camp along the main trail. While I could not make out the details of their banner, I was able to see they were riding beneath a Roman standard. My breath caught in my throat, with a rush of blood slamming into my temples as the floodgate in my heart banged in my chest to release its liquid force. I was almost dizzy with the pleasurable thought of revenge. Hiram must have seen what I was looking at and read my thoughts as he offered,

"My friend, things like this must be thought through. You cannot go about this on feelings of revenge alone, you must think and plan."

"I can't let him get away."

"Where is he going to go my friend, that you will not also be there?"

Hiram was right, I couldn't just go barging down into a Roman encampment bent on the idea of killing the Roman who had extinguished my very life. Besides, except for a name, I had no idea which Roman was the one I was looking for. I had to have a plan, but what? Again Hiram seemed to read my mind.

"Barabbas, I know I shouldn't get involved in your situation but without a plan, you cannot succeed. I will help you get into the Roman camp and help you find Gaucius."

I was starting to feel a great kinship with Hiram and vowed to myself if I made it through what I was about to undertake, I would make a blood oath to be there to assist him in whatever endeavor he may need me for, for the rest of my life.

Hiram's plan was simple enough yet effective if the Roman's past desire to purchase a knife was still evident. We slowly made our way into the encampment and were quickly stopped by two Legionnaires.

"And what do we have here? Two wandering infidels. Why have you come to a Roman camp, are you offering yourselves up for slaughter, or are we to assume you have business with us?" One of the Legionnaires asked.

"We are vendors from Lydda." Hiram offered. "We have followed you because one of your men, a Gaucius I think his name is, was interested in a knife we have and we have decided to sell it, that is, if he still wants to buy it."

"And what makes you think there would be a Gaucius here?" The Legionnaire asked, eyeing us suspiciously.

"I saw the rest of your Legion go back toward Jerusalem, but Gaucius mentioned he had business to tend to in Joppa." Hiram countered.

"You realize of course, with the information you have, you could be called a spy in which case we would have to arrest you, or even put you to death."

"We are not spies," Hiram stated confidently yet angrily. "If we can not do business with Gaucius, we will be on our way."

The Legionnaire stared at us for what seemed an eternity. Finally, he instructed a colleague to announce to Gaucius that we sought a meeting with him.

A short time later, a very tall and rugged-looking Roman stood before us. His hair was longer than normally allowed by the Legion and his eyes carried a sleepy almost non-caring look about them. A ragged scar that made its way from his right temple area to the right corner of his mouth commanded attention and put him on the defensive immediately.

"You see something about me that interests you?" Gaucius spit out.

"No, only that I hope you are still interested in the ebony handled knife you asked about," Hiram answered.

"Well, well, so now you want to sell it. What changed your mind? You told me you could never part with it and now you come begging me to buy it?" Gaucius said with what looked like a ghastly smile.

"I have not come begging. Should you not be interested I can assure you I can find another buyer. I gave it some thought and realized there was no real reason not to sell it as I have many knives and I wanted to see what offer you would make."

"Well now, seeing how I had not given it any more thought and wasn't looking to buy it now, my price would be cheaper than I originally had planned on paying." The Legionnaire stated in an obvious bartering mode. "Let's see, I guess I am willing to pay two shekels for it."

"Two shekels? I wouldn't sell my donkey's dung for two shekels, make it ten and you can have it." Hiram bartered.

"Ten? You must be crazy from your travels, the blade is chipped and it looks like it won't hold an edge, but since you tire me I"ll make it three and a half shekels."

"This knife has the finest of ebony for a handle and will easily cut your long hair so you meet Roman regulations. Nine shekels and not a shekel less."

"We are wasting both of our time. I do not have nine shekels. All I have is four shekels and I know you won't sell it to me for that, but I do have something that you may be interested in."

The Legionnaire reached inside his tunic and pulled out a goat-skin pouch. Opening the pouch he extracted an object that immediately forced me to catch my breath and anger.

"Take a look at this, this is an armlet the Samaritan women wear. Look at the fine quality and the way the stones capture the light." The Roman said, displaying a small yet beautiful armlet.

I recognized the armlet immediately as the one I had purchased for Rebekah on another buying mission I had made to Cana. Because of its beauty, I had bought it to compliment Rebekah's very own beauty.

Looking at the armlet in the Legionnaire's hand was almost more than I could stand, but I knew I could not attack him now, with his colleagues standing nearby, no, this was going to take strategy.

"That is a pretty nice piece of work you have there, you say it is Egyptian?" Hiram asked.

"I said no such thing. I don't know if it's Egyptian or not, all I know is I got it from some whore in Nain. So what, do we have a deal or not? I'll give you four shekels and the armlet for the knife." The Roman offered impatiently.

"We have a deal." Hiram agreed. After shaking the Roman's hand, he handed the knife over and the Roman gave him the money and armlet. Hiram was quick to lead me away from the Legionnaire.

"Calm yourself! You can do nothing right now."

"What are you talking about?" I asked absently as I watched the Roman disappear inside of a tent admiring his newly acquired knife.

"I realized as soon as he said he got the armlet in Nain that it may have some meaning to you. It does, doesn't it?" Hiram asked.

"It was Rebekah's. I bought it for her on a previous trip to Cana. She accompanied me on that trip and as soon as I saw it, I realized I had to buy it for her because it would accentuate her beauty."

"Ah yes, so now you have more of a reason to kill him with your own hands, do you not?"

"Oh, I am going to kill him alright!"

"Yes, but how, that's the question and I can assure you until you have that figured out, do not attempt it. Killing him and then getting yourself killed will accomplish nothing, but to kill him and live to tell about it may heal a lot." Hiram philosophized.

"You're right of course, my friend."

But how do I get him by himself and how do I do it in a way that they won't come after us? I pondered out loud. At that moment a plan came to mind, but it was going to rely on assistance from Hiram and I wasn't sure I wanted to get him involved any further.

"So, Barabbas how are you going to do it?" Hiram asked me as we sat around an early evening campfire.

"Do what?" I asked non-committedly.

"How do you plan to dispatch the Roman?"

"The less you know Hiram, the better off you are," I warned.

"Oh come now, if you end up killing him and I have to believe that is your plan, what makes you think the Legion is going to come after only you? We both came here and asked for Gaucius, he is killed and they are only going to come after you? Make sense, man. I'm as involved in any plan you have and as such, I have a right to know what the plan is that will ultimately get me killed, don't you think so?"

Despite myself, I had to smile and agree that what he said made plenty of sense. If I were going to kill the Roman, Hiram was going to be equally blamed because of his relationship with me so I might as well enlist his help.

After admitting I wanted to come up with a plan to lure the Roman away from his colleagues, Hiram turned out to be an excellent planner on such details. After working out all the plans for our mission, we went back into town to hatch it.

CHAPTER FIFTEEN

FINDING AN INN THAT *had many boisterous drunkards lounging about we knew we would find what we were looking for. Finding the inn's proprietor, we asked if any of his girls were available. Lecherously smiling he charged us three times the amount no doubt assuming the two of us were going to indulge in the woman's services at the same time. Not desiring to waste time and effort correcting his misconception, we paid the money and found the woman.*

Sarah was her name and while she was anything but pretty, the thickly applied makeup did an adequate job of covering up her obvious facial flaws. We had to hope a Legionnaire of Gaucius' stature would not care what her face looked like.

Sarah was no friend of Romans. When we first explained that she was to seduce one, she began crying and said she wanted nothing to do with our plan. We assured her that we would not let him hurt her and that we would be willing to pay her ten times the amount she ordinarily charged for her services. Finally, she said she would help us.

Hiram and I went to the edge of town where the mountains began and hid behind an outcropping of rocks waiting for Sarah to perform her act.

We didn't have long to wait. Sarah's part in our plan was to walk up to the Roman's tent unseen and call to him, when he answered, she was to beckon him with her services. Naturally, he would want her to come into his tent, but she would explain to him that she wanted only to service him and that their sounds of love would draw the attention of his colleagues. She was to suggest they go to the edge of town and make love nestled among the boulders under the nighttime stars.

Sarah performed her job perfectly. It appeared the Roman was so enraptured with her he was unaware of our hiding just behind him. We were close enough that had he not been breathing so hard, he would have heard our breath.

Sarah seductively began to loosen her clothing which only inflamed the Roman to tear at his uniform in a hasty attempt to undress. We watched as he struggled with a boot and decided that was the time in which to pounce.

Before Gaucius could yell out, Hiram had leaped upon him and had an arm firmly around the Roman's neck. When the realization came that he was under attack, the Roman began to struggle and twist in the attempt to throw Hiram off, but his violent twisting only served to cause their legs to become entangled and they fell to the ground.

Following our instructions, Sarah ran back to the inn and was not to leave or tell anyone what was going on. She had been paid well and was further promised additional pay when we came back.

Leaping out of the darkness, I joined the fray and succeeded in hitting the Roman several times to the front of his head with a fairly large rock. Eventually, Gaucius went slack and Hiram was able to let go of the chokehold he had used. Checking to be sure Gaucius was not dead, we went to work tying him up with some used ropes from old fishing nets. After firmly securing the Legionnaire, we sat down to wait for him to awaken.

Hiram suggested that we simply take him to the top of the mountain, untie him and shove him over the cliff, and while that sounded compelling, I was more interested in hearing from the Roman himself that he had killed my family and why. Once I had those answers, I assured him we would again knock him out and throw him off the mountain.

Growing impatient at watching the Roman sleep what looked like a peaceful sleep, I got up from the small campfire we had built and threw some water on his face. Sputtering, Gaucius quickly sat up and appeared to strain against the rope that firmly held him. Watching him look around, you could see he was assessing his situation and then his eyes fixed on us.

"So, getting paid for the knife wasn't enough, you're thieves and want to rob me, huh? Well, I hate to disappoint you, but I don't have any money on me." Gaucius stated smugly.

"We're not thieves and there's nothing you have that we want, that is except for some answers," I intoned.

"Answers to what? What do you want to know, how you're both going to die? Do you think you can do this to a Legionnaire and live?"

"For a man who is in such an awkward position, you sure speak like a fool, Gaucius. Can you not see your life is in our hands? We currently are in the position to decide if you will live or die." Hiram added.

"Okay, let's cut out all this small talk. You have me here in this position for a reason. What is it you want money, food, are you slaves and want freedom, what? What do you want?"

"I already told you, we want some answers. At least he does." Hiram said pointing toward me.

"And what questions should I be answering for you and why should I answer them?"

"For one, I began coolly. Answering my questions will allow you to live just that much longer. The longer and more in-depth your answers are, the longer you live."

"Alright, I'll play along, what's your question?"

"Very good. First question, the armlet you paid for the knife with, again tell me where did you get it from? I asked.

"Like I already told you, I got it from some whore in Nain."

It was all I could do not to pull my knife out and cut his throat, but I had to have some answers, and killing him would have to wait.

"And did this whore have a little boy with her?"

"I don't remember, maybe. Why?"

"And did you kill this whore and the boy?"

"Who are you and what kind of questions are these?"

"After you killed them did you burn their house down?"

"Who is this guy?" The Roman asked Hiram. Hiram simply shrugged and remained silent.

I got up, stepped over to the seated Gaucius looming over him. Looking up at me by the firelight, you could see the fear beginning to form on his face.

"Did they beg you not to hurt them, not to kill them, Gaucius? Did the boy try to defend his mother? Well, did he? Did he Gaucius!?" As I screamed the last question I lifted my sandaled foot and planted a well-placed kick squarely across Gaucius' mouth. He fell back and blood began to flow freely from his broken maw.

Groggily sitting back up smiling, Gaucius spit out two teeth I had kicked out.

"Okay, now you've sealed your fate. You kidnap a Roman Legionnaire, and then you put your foot on me? You are going to die and die a horrible death, I can assure you of that."

"That doesn't matter, Gaucius, I've been dead for a long time now. When you killed my wife and son, you killed me, so I have nothing to lose. I can assure you before I am through with you, you will wish you were dead."

"You don't scare me, swine, and just so you'll know, I enjoyed your wife. As a matter-of-fact, I killed her when she wouldn't let go of me. She really enjoyed my company. What a filthy woman, but when you're away from civilized society and desperate, anything will . . . ."

He never got to finish the statement as I picked up a forearm-sized piece of firewood and began beating him over and over on his head.

With each strike of the club I now wielded, pieces of Gaucius' flesh opened and scarlet streams began to flow freely down his head, and yet I couldn't stop. Again and again, I struck him, and with each blow, exhilaration similar to drunkenness filled me so that I toned down the force of each blow only so I could prolong this monster's death.

A few more swings and I had to stop. I had used up too much energy too quickly and could just stand there looking down at Gaucius' broken head. Pained groans escaped from somewhere in the Roman's body and then he did something I was sure would be impossible - he sat up and through broken lips, smiled.

"Killing the boy was the best." Gaucius blubbered through blood-soaked lips. "He thought he could stop me from having fun with your whore. I delighted in impaling him on my spear like lamb on a spit and roasting him in the fire I set, all under the watchful eye of his mother. I made sure she watched before I killed her too." This was followed by a crazed sadistic laugh.

Easing my knife from the folds of my robe, I grabbed Gaucius' long hair and violently snapped his head back revealing a dirt-encrusted off-white throat, seeming to beg me to cut it. I could see the carotid beating hysterically beneath the skin.

A smile crept over my face as I prepared to draw the blade slowly across Gaucius' neck. I had sharpened the blade enough that it adequately sheared sheep, yet dull enough to make the process of cutting flesh agonizing.

As I was preparing to cut Gaucius' throat, my arm was held tight effectively keeping the knife from reaching the supple tissue of Gaucius' neck. The smile faded from my face as I turned to see Hiram holding my arm.

"No Barabbas, no. If we kill him now, like this, we are doomed."

"You're doomed anyway fools. Do you think you can get away with . . . ?" Gaucius began.

Gaucius was cut off in mid-sentence by a well-placed foot to his plexus by Hiram's foot. All Gaucius could do was double over with blood and now spittle cascading from his broken mouth.

This allowed me to see that Hiram was right, but how could we dispatch Gaucius without drawing attention to our plot?

My answer came as I looked about the countryside. Right behind us was the mountain range we had ascended earlier. Just before its peak, along a sheer face, was an outcropping from which a drop or fall would be right down onto the boulders we now stood amongst. A drop from that height was certain death.

It was like Hiram read my mind as he smiled.

"Now you're thinking, Barabbas. At least then we can make it look like he fell."

Grabbing the Roman by his hair, I began to pull him violently toward the mountain. When a significant plug of his hair came out in my hands, I quit and looked at Hiram. With one of us on either side of Gaucius, we were able to half drag and half carry him up the mountain. After the toil of the climb, combined with my anger, I was all for taking him to the edge and kicking him over, but something inside me said, "wait." So I stopped.

Looking down at the unconscious Gaucius, I found it hard to recognize any features that would distinguish who he was. It was then, that I remembered a similar situation of not being able to recognize the victim of a savage beating. It hadn't been so long ago that Jesus stood before Pilate covered in blood unrecognizable. I began to feel a little pity for Gaucius, and then another part of me said "throw him to his death. Remember what he did to your family."

With Hiram watching me from a distance, I grabbed Gaucius beneath both shoulders and struggled to drag him to the cliff's edge. Hiram slowly walked over and gently touched my shoulder.

"Barabbas, is it really worth it? Will it bring them back or remove the sadness and pain over your loss?

"So what am I supposed to do Hiram?" I was crying now. "Just let him go? Forget what he did to my family?"

"Yes Barabbas, that is what I am saying. I know you didn't know this and, I know you are not, but I too am a follower of Jesus, a Christian and I know he would not approve of us taking another's life for our vengeful purposes."

"You, you knew Jesus?" I asked in shock.

"I didn't know him personally but knew of him and I know he would not want this."

"He wouldn't want it?" I asked incredulously. "Why would I care what a dead Jew would want?"

With tears openly flowing from my eyes, I renewed my efforts dragging Gaucius to the cliff's edge. Finally getting him close enough to easily kick him over, I decided I wanted him awake just before and as he was falling to his death. I wanted him to experience terror as I am sure Rebekah and Dodavah had.

Taking one of the fishnet ropes Hiram had packed in my provisions, I cut a small portion to tie around Gaucius' wrists. The rest I used to tie his ankles together, with just enough left to leave him dangling over the cliff's edge until I was ready to release it and drop him to his death.

Retrieving a gourd filled with water, I began pouring it onto Gaucius' face until he sputtered awake. Gaucius looked around and I delighted in seeing him register what I felt was a look of terror as realization must have sat in. Using my feet, I prodded and pushed Gaucius closer to the cliff's edge. This was made harder because of his violent twisting and squirming, but I finally succeeded in getting him precariously close to the edge, close enough that if his eyes were open, Gaucius could see the drop he was about to make. It was then an unmistakable smell of fear permeated the air. Urine. Gaucius' bladder had released its foul contents. At almost the same instant, a blood-curdling scream or maybe a terrified cry elevated from his lungs providing me with an instance of pure joy.

Holding tightly the free end of the rope I quickly pushed the screaming Gaucius over the edge. As the slack in the rope depleted leaving a taut band, for a moment I feared Gaucius' weight would pull me over the cliff as well, but I quickly found a boulder from which to stand behind and prop my feet against it.

The next few minutes were a blur and cacophony of voices. Gaucius was screaming for his life, Hiram was begging me not to do it, and commingled in this symphony was a voice I knew was inside my head but sounded so loud I was sure Hiram could hear it as well. The voice was very calm in stark contrast to the others and beautiful, almost melodic in its tone and temperament.

"Barabbas, remember how the crowd clamored for me to be sacrificed so that you may live? There were two who were sacrificed as well, that Gaucius may live as well." I tried shaking my head to rid it of the voice and screamed, "Nooooo, he killed them and must die!"

"And you are the judge of that?" The voice continued. "You who have killed many. You who have stolen much. You who would have been put to death if not for another, you will judge this man?"

It was at that precise moment Gaucius' voice broke through my conscious, "Oh God, help me. I'm sorry. I don't want to die!"

I don't know if his plea was sincere or to what god he now begged, but something stirred inside me. Looking at the edge from which Gaucius dangled, I saw what appeared to be a bright light in the form of a man standing there, yet no humanly characteristics were discernible.

"Who are you?" I asked.

"You know who I am," the voice inside my head answered. "To judge and kill this man would doom you to suffer forever. You were given a second chance, is not Gaucius worthy of the same? There is a need for both of you."

And then the voice was gone, and just like that renewed clarity began oozing back and I could hear Gaucius' continued apologies and Hiram's frantic begging of me not to do it.

Something inside me felt broken and I began to cry, a cry that seemed to contain all my hurt, all my sorrow, and yet, a feeling of newness. Gaucius let out another blood-curdling scream just as the rope, which held him suspended from death, began to slip through my hands.

"Hiram! I yelled. Help me! The rope, I can't hold it anymore. Help me pull him up."

Hiram ran toward me and grabbed the last few centimeters of rope as it left my hands. Quickly shaking my arms to restore the blood circulation, I once again grabbed the taut hemp cord and helped Hiram pull Gaucius, ever so slowly, back up and over the edge again, onto the safety of a solid surface.

The three of us just laid there exhausted, spent, with no further thought of revenge or getting even. Each of us had experienced a life-changing moment and could only now cherish what it meant. Finally, still panting, Gaucius broke the silence.

"Why? Why did you bring me back up?"

"It's funny, I began. All I could think of since I found out you murdered my family was killing you at all cost."

"And what changed? All you had to do was release the rope and it would have been over. You'd have your revenge and . . . ?"

"But nothing would change. Killing you would not bring them back." I responded.

"I hope you don't think because you pulled me back up it changes anything. You're still a criminal wanted by the Empire and you'll have to face Pilate."

"And you're still a murderous Roman Legionnaire, and you'll have to answer for your criminal act someday." I intoned.

"Answer to who?" Gaucius asked half laughing.

"You'll have to answer for all you've done wrong in your life before the Lord someday and . . . ."

"Before the Lord? And which Lord are you speaking of, one of our Roman gods, Caesar himself, or perhaps you speak of a Greek god - Zeus, Isis, which one will I have to speak before?"

"None of them, they are not gods. You will have to answer before Jesus someday!"

I spoke confidently. I was stunned, I had not planned on saying that, but now that it was out, I was determined to stick with it.

Hiram's head shot up. He had been looking at the rope burns on his hands when I answered Gaucius. His eyes met mine for a few seconds, but in that short time, I could see he knew what I was talking about. A knowing twinkle from his eyes was directed at me and I returned it with a smile I hoped would convey that I too believed.

"The Jew we crucified?" Gaucius asked, mystified. "You're telling me that you believe he is a god and I'll answer to him?"

Hiram and I didn't answer; we just stood there staring at the Roman.

"Oh come on, you can't be serious, a god? I've heard other Legionnaires who hunted him say he was different, even some who said they couldn't understand why the Empire was wasting so much effort on him, but none of them mentioned anything about him being godly. As a matter-of-fact, they say he was just another

Jewish carpenter from the rundown town of Nazareth. Nothing more, nothing less."

"That may be the Roman opinion and you are entitled to it," I answered. "But, as a follower of Jesus - a Christian, I am compelled to tell you I, Barabbas, a convert, forgive you in the name of Jesus."

"And I Hiram, also a follower of Jesus, forgive you for taking part in the plight of your fellow humans." Hiram was beaming with what appeared to be a visible joy.

"Okay, so what now? You both forgive me, but now what?" Gaucius asked suspiciously.

"You're free to go, Gaucius," I answered. "As for me, I now go to spread the word of the Lord to everyone I come into contact with. Hiram, what about you?"

"Well, if you don't mind, this part of the country has grown too predictable for me, so if you could use the company, I'd like to tag along," Hiram started smiling.

"You realize, of course, your mission will be quite short. The Empire will never stop looking for you and you'll end up dead just like your friend, Jesus." Gaucius interrupted.

"What a nice thing to say, your friend, Jesus." He is our friend and yours too Gaucius. I offered.

"Yeah well, I think you're both crazy. So I'm free to go?"

Both Hiram and I nodded he could go. Wasting no time, Gaucius quickly grabbed his helmet and began making his way down the mountain.

Hiram and I gathered our things; the gourd, rope, and sack with loaves of bread, and slowly followed the path we had taken up. Both of us were quiet, consumed by our thoughts, of the events over the past three days, anticipating what was to come.

"Hey, Barabbas!" A voice echoed from below us. "You saved my life today and that's worth something to me. I can't stop Pilate from looking for you but I also have never seen you. That's the best I can do. I still think you're crazy, but good luck."

"Thank you Gaucius, and good luck to you as well." I replied.

I never heard anything more concerning Gaucius but he kept his word because the Romans seemed to have given up on capturing me. As for Hiram and I, we made it to Joppa and found a very rapt group of young people anxious to learn as much as they could concerning Jesus. When they learned I was the Barabbas, that was saved that Jesus could be crucified, they seemed to hold me in some form of strange reverence because I had been in the presence of Jesus. It took a great effort to explain that I was not worthy of the adulation they misguidedly directed toward me.

Once they realized I was just like them and in some cases, more flawed, they relaxed and removed me from the pinnacle they had placed me on.

Chapter Sixteen

Finally, the day arrived when Hiram and I were to go to Greece. We knew not what lied ahead, but we were both certain we had a mission there. The urge to spread the word of Jesus' teachings to others grew stronger in us daily and we couldn't wait to get started. Our excitement reached a level I didn't think possible when we learned that one of Jesus' disciples had gone to Greece before us. Peter had had a vision in which the Lord told him that the teachings must be presented to the Gentile as well, and had gone to heed the call.

Hiram nodded in agreement when I suggested we find Peter and join up with him and assist in spreading the word. Needless to say, our excitement grows in leaps and bounds with anticipation. Who knows when or where this journey will end, but until it does, I will continue to spread the word of Jesus.